Erle Stanley Gardner

The Case of the

Queenly Contestant

HEINEMANN : LONDON

William Heinemann Ltd
15 Queen Street, Mayfair, London W1X 8BE

LONDON MELBOURNE TORONTO
JOHANNESBURG AUCKLAND

Printed Offset Litho and bound in Great Britain
by Cox & Wyman Ltd,
London, Fakenham and Reading

Foreword

Professor Leon Derobert is internationally known and respected for his work in the field of legal medicine.

I have, from time to time, commented in my books about the importance of legal medicine and its function in the detection of crime.

We hear so much about the efficiency of science in detecting crimes that too few people realize what a sad state of affairs results when science is absent in this field. And, yet, science almost always is absent unless there is some regularly qualified expert in forensic medicine to take charge of the investigation.

Many times wounds of entrance in the case of a gunshot are considered wounds of exit. Many times death by poisoning is mistaken for a natural death.

I have tried in these Perry Mason books to impress upon my readers who are interested in crime (and many of whom are first-class amateur detectives) the importance of supporting a program of legal medicine.

And so it gives me great pleasure to dedicate this book to my friend, PROFESSOR LEON DEROBERT.

—ERLE STANLEY GARDNER

5

THE CASE OF THE

Queenly Contestant

Chapter One

DELLA STREET, Perry Mason's confidential secretary, answered the telephone, talked briefly with the receptionist, then turned to Perry Mason.

"There is a woman in the outer office who gives her name simply as Ellen Adair. She says she knows it is an imposition to try to see you without an appointment, but she is prepared to pay you anything within reason. She has to see you right away on a matter of the greatest urgency, and she's very agitated."

Mason glanced at his wristwatch and at the papers on which he was working.

Della Street, looking at the appointment book, said hopefully, "You have twenty-eight minutes until your next appointment."

"I wanted to have this legal point digested before that time," Mason said, then shrugged. "Oh, well, I guess we have to take care of the urgent matters. Go take a look,

Della, and size her up. Find out what she wants to see me about."

Della nodded, said into the telephone, "Tell her that I'll be right out, Gertie."

Della Street left the office to return within a couple of minutes.

"Well?" Mason asked.

"She gets me," Della Street said. "She's a tall woman in her late thirties or perhaps early forties. Her clothes are quiet, modest, and expensive. Her bearing is regal—that of someone who is accustomed to giving orders. She's two or three inches taller than I am and well formed."

"And what does she want to see me about?" Mason asked.

"She wants to ask you some questions about law," Della said. "She says the questions will be purely academic and impersonal."

Mason sighed. "Another one of these cases where a client tries to hide behind a shield of anonymity. She'll come in and say, 'Suppose A marries B and B inherits property from his mother in New Mexico. Suppose A and B are having a divorce. Can A claim one-half of the property?' Oh, I know the whole rigmarole, Della."

Della extended a fifty-dollar bill. "She has given me fifty dollars as a retainer."

Mason hesitated a moment, then said, "Give it back to her. Tell her that I'll talk with her briefly: that if I decide to answer her questions, I'll make a reasonable charge; that if I can't satisfy myself she is putting her cards face up on the table, she had better get another attorney."

"She says there is no time to get another attorney, that

she simply has to see you, and that action has to be taken immediately."

"I see," Mason said. "She wants to ask me a lot of academic law questions and then take action. Oh, well, Della, she's a human being, she's in trouble of some sort, so let's find out what it's all about. Bring her in."

Della Street nodded, left the office, and returned within a matter of seconds with a woman who stood very erect and held her head back and her chin up in an imperious manner. She bowed to Mason, said, "Mr. Mason, thank you for seeing me," walked over to the client's chair, calmly seated herself, and said, "Please pay very careful attention to what I am about to say, Mr. Mason, because we are fighting against time and I have to know where I stand."

"And what's the trouble?" Mason asked.

She shook her head. "Let me ask the questions, please. Mr. Mason, I have heard something about the right of privacy. Can you tell me what it is?"

"The right of privacy," Mason said, "has been defined as the right of a person to be left alone."

"That means he is immune from publicity?"

"No," Mason said, "like every other doctrine of law, it is subject to exceptions. Perhaps if you'd tell me just what is bothering you, I could save a lot of time. A dissertation on the law of privacy would consume a lot of time, and some of the information I would be giving you would be irrelevant."

"Such as what?" she asked. "Please tell me quickly what are the exceptions."

Mason said, "If you are walking along the street in a

public place and a photographer takes your picture to illustrate a street scene, he can use that picture as a magazine illustration.

"If the photographer singles you out to take your particular picture, he may or may not still be within his rights. If he uses that picture for any commercial enterprise, he has violated your privacy.

"If, on the other hand, you become newsworthy because you are the victim of a holdup, or if you decide to run for public office, or if you do anything of your own volition which makes you newsworthy . . ."

"I see. I see," she said, looking at her watch impatiently. "You're right. I'm going at it in the wrong way. A person who runs for public office waives the right of privacy?"

"Within reasonable limitations, yes."

"How about a person who runs for—well, a beauty contest?"

"Declaring herself as a candidate?" Mason asked.

"Yes."

"The same situation would apply."

"And how long would that situation last?"

"At least as long as the contest and the enjoyment of the rewards of the contest, if any.

"Understand, Miss Adair—or is it Mrs. Adair?"

"It's *Miss* Adair," the woman said sharply. "Ellen Adair."

"All right. Understand, Miss Adair, this is a relatively new branch of the law. From its very nature it is not capable of exact, precise delineation. Each case depends largely on the facts in that particular case.

"Now let me suggest that, if you're involved in anything where you wish to assert your right to privacy, you start in, in an orderly way, by telling me the facts of the case and quit beating around the bush.

"After I have the facts I can apply my knowledge of the law to the facts and give you an intelligent answer.

"If you try to get the law from me and then apply the law to the facts, you may make a very costly mistake. You might know the legal principle, but the application to a particular set of facts would be all wrong."

She hesitated, bit her lip, frowned, averted her eyes, then, reaching a sudden decision, turned to Mason and said, "Very well; twenty years ago in a Midwestern city I was a contestant in one of those bathing-beauty contests. I won first prize. I was eighteen at the time. Winning the contest went to my head. I thought I was a motion-picture star, because winning the contest gave me a free trip to Hollywood and a screen test by one of the major studios."

"You came to Hollywood and took the test?" Mason asked.

"Yes."

"And have been here ever since?"

Ellen Adair shook her head. "No," she said, "I disappeared."

"Disappeared?" Mason asked, his voice showing his interest.

"Yes."

"Why?"

"To have my baby," she said.

There were several seconds of silence, then Mason said sympathetically, "Go on."

"Now," she said, "a paper in my hometown is publishing one of those features which the rural newspapers dig up from time to time: a column dealing with twenty-five years ago, twenty years ago, fifteen years ago, ten years ago."

"I see," Mason said noncommittally.

"Well, they want to publish a story about me winning the beauty prize twenty years ago, it was quite an honor for the town. I won the state beauty contest, and the hometown was proud of me.

"Then I went to Hollywood and had a screen test and nothing came of it. I was given an automobile, a motion-picture camera, a projector, a lot of beauty creams and toilet articles, an airplane trip to Las Vegas—all that type of thing which is showered on a girl who wins a contest and from which the manufacturers get enough publicity so it offsets the cost of the merchandise. It is, of course, all part of a commercialized advertising program, and I was too dumb to know it. I thought that I was getting all of those things because of my popularity and charm."

"And then you disappeared?" Mason said.

"Abruptly," she said. "I wrote friends that I had a flattering offer to go to Europe. Of course I didn't go to Europe."

"Quite obviously," Mason said, "this is a painful interview for you. It is raking over the ashes of a dead past, but it is also apparent that you are faced with a very real emergency. Does the newspaper know where you are now?"

"It can find me."

"How?"

"It's rather a long story. I disappeared. I didn't even let my family know where I was. Remember that this was twenty years ago. The whole mores of the people have changed materially in twenty years. An unmarried woman can have a baby now and get by with it if she's clever and self-respecting. In those days it was a matter of deep shame—shame to the unwed mother, shame to the parents, shame to the community.

"The whole town where I lived was proud of me. That would have changed overnight. They would have crucified me on a cross of public scorn."

"No need to explain all that," Mason said. "As a lawyer I know the facts of life. But you disappeared. You didn't let your folks know where you were?"

"No."

"And what happened?"

"My father died. My mother married again. Then her second husband died, and a few months ago my mother died. She left an estate of some fifty thousand dollars and no heirs. She left a will stating that the money was all to go to me if I was still alive and if I could be found."

"Your mother was still living in this little town," Mason asked, "where she . . . ?"

"No, she had moved to Indianapolis. I had several . . . well, I had kept myself advised of what she was doing and where she was living. I would send her Christmas cards and birthday cards with no signature on them, but I think she knew whom they were from all right.

"Anyhow, I employed an attorney in Indianapolis, went there, established my identity, and collected the money. No one connected me with the winner of the bathing-beauty contest twenty years ago."

"And what makes you think you could be connected with the past now?" Mason asked.

She said, "In twenty years the little town where I lived has become a fairly big city. The evening paper, *The Cloverville Gazette,* is a bustling, enterprising, aggressive newspaper.

"It has been publishing a series of articles on what happened twenty-five years ago, twenty years ago, fifteen years ago, and it has asked its readers for suggestions, follow-ups on old news stories that they think would be of interest to the readers.

"A few days ago a reader sent in this letter," she said. "It speaks for itself."

She opened her purse and took out a newspaper clipping and handed it to the lawyer.

Mason read the clipping aloud:

"Twenty years ago this city was signally honored by having one of its residents chosen as the most beautiful young woman in the entire state.

"Ellen Calvert brought great honors to this city. Her dazzling beauty made an impression not only locally but in Hollywood. Then, at the height of her popularity, she went to Europe on what was supposed to be the start of a stage career.

"Nothing ever came of the stage career. It would be interesting to know where Ellen Calvert is today, what she is doing, how the world has been using her.

"Ellen Calvert's father died. Her mother, Estelle, moved away, and rumor is that she remarried.

"What is the real story of Ellen Calvert? Is it the story of a beautiful woman whose beauty was such that she outgrew the small community in which she lived, outgrew her local friends, moved on into wider circles and achieved success? Or is it the story of a young woman who was dazzled by success, was led to believe the world was her oyster, and then was plunged into the depths of disappointment?

"Readers everywhere would be interested in getting the sequel to this interesting story of twenty years ago."

Mason handed the newspaper clipping back to his client. "When," he asked, "did you take the name of Ellen Adair?"

"When I disappeared."

"Some of my questions," Mason said, "have to be somewhat embarrassing. Was the father of your child named Adair?"

Her lips tightened. She shook her head. "There are certain things, Mr. Mason, we are *not* going into."

"You feel that the newspaper can locate you?"

"Unfortunately, yes. If the newspaper starts digging, it will find that my mother married Henry Leland Berry, that after her death I showed up and identified myself as her daughter and claimed the money.

"You can imagine how I felt, Mr. Mason. I had been ashamed to keep in touch with my mother during the period when the knowledge of what had happened would have been a terrific blow to her and to the family pride.

"After her death it seemed selfish to appear and claim the money, but if I hadn't it would have gone to the state because there were no other heirs."

"And what you want is to kill this story. Is that right?"

"That's right."

Mason said, "If I appear in the matter, the newspaper will naturally suppose that you are located somewhere in this vicinity."

"There are several million people located somewhere in this vicinity," she said.

"You don't think they can trace you?"

"There is only one way they can trace me," she said, "and that is through the Indianapolis trail—and the newspaper simply has to be stopped before they start following that trail."

Mason nodded to Della Street. "Get me the managing editor of *The Cloverville Gazette* on the line, Della."

"Shall I tell them who's calling?" Della Street asked.

Mason nodded. "Better put the call through from the switchboard in the outer office, Della."

Della Street nodded, went out to give the call to Gertie at the switchboard.

When she had gone, Mason said to his client, "You have reason to believe there is something more behind all this than just the desire on the part of some reader to dig into the past and find out what happened to you as a beauty-contest winner?"

She nodded.

"Care to tell me what it is?" Mason asked.

"I don't think that is necessary," she said. "Are you going to tell the editor of the paper that I am a client of yours?"

"Not in so many words," Mason said.

Della Street returned to the office. "The call is going through," she said.

"Della," Mason said, "give Ellen Adair a dollar bill."

Della Street glanced at Mason quizzically.

Mason indicated the petty-cash drawer.

Della opened it, took out a dollar bill, gravely handed it to Ellen Adair.

"Now then," Mason said, "Della Street is a resident of Hollywood who is thinking of producing a play. She may want to give you a part in that play. She . . ."

The telephone rang.

Della Street picked up the receiver, nodded to Mason.

"Hello," Mason said, "is this the managing editor of *The Cloverville Gazette*? . . . I see. I'm Perry Mason, an attorney in Los Angeles, and I am representing a Hollywood party who is interested in a deal with Ellen Calvert, who was the subject of an article which appeared a short time ago in your paper."

"Well, well, well," the voice at the other end of the line said, "this is indeed an honor. We're attracting attention quite far away from our local sphere of influence."

"You are, indeed," Mason said. "Have you got anywhere with the story of Ellen Calvert?"

"We're doing some research. We've got some very fine photographs of her when she won the contest. There was a banquet by the Chamber of Commerce—lots of copy. We've got photographs and files and . . ."

"Kill it!" Mason said.

"What was that?"

"I said kill it!"

"I'm afraid I don't understand what you mean," the managing editor said.

"I mean kill it. Take your men off it. Forget it. Stop it. Don't touch it with a ten-foot pole," Mason said.

"May I ask why not?"

"Primarily because I'm telling you not to touch it. If you do, you're going to get into a whole mess of trouble."

"We are not accustomed to having the editorial policies of this newspaper dictated by persons who ring up and make threats."

"I'm not making threats," Mason said, "and I have no desire to intimidate you. I'm simply representing a client and taking the first step which is necessary to protect the interests of that client—to wit, telling you to kill the story.

"Now then, you probably have some attorney who represents you. I would much prefer to deal direct with your attorney. I will explain to him the legal reasons back of the position I am taking."

"If you could tell me the legal reason, if you could give me just one good legal reason," the editor said, "I'd feel a lot different about all this."

"Ever heard about the invasion of privacy?" Mason asked.

"What newspaperman hasn't?" the editor said. "Although I understand it's rather hazy as far as the legal applications are concerned. But the doctrine is well known."

"Well," Mason said, "the law of invasion of privacy protects a person against having her privacy invaded. It is the right of a person to be let alone."

"Now just a minute," the editor said. "I'm no lawyer, but there are certain exceptions to this rule. When a person becomes newsworthy, the right of privacy no longer exists. When a person deliberately puts himself in a position where he is newsworthy, the doctrine . . ."

"Don't waste my time telling *me* the law," Mason said. "Ask your attorney to call me on the phone."

"Do you dispute the legal points I am making?" the editor asked.

"Certainly not," Mason said. "Those legal points are all right, but after the particular events which made a person newsworthy have terminated, the right of privacy again exists."

"I'm afraid I don't follow you," the editor said.

"If the cashier of your local bank embezzled a hundred thousand dollars, that would be news," Mason said. "You could publish photographs of the embezzler. You could cover the trial of the embezzler. You could cover the sentence.

"After the sentence had expired, after the embezzler had paid his debt to society and been released, if he went into business under another name, you couldn't ferret him out, publish the story of his defalcation and his subsequent rehabilitation as news. That would be an invasion of privacy."

"Yes, I suppose so," the editor said, "but surely that's not the case here. This is the case of a very beautiful young woman of whom the community is proud. There is nothing shameful about winning a beauty contest."

"Publish all you want to about her winning the beauty contest," Mason said, "but don't go in for any twenty-year follow-up. I wish you'd have your attorney call me."

"No, no, no," the editor said, "that's not going to be necessary, Mr. Mason. If you adopt this position, we aren't going to consider the story important enough to risk a lawsuit. You say you're representing a Hollywood producer? May I ask if Ellen Calvert is perhaps making a success in films—possibly under another name?"

"You may not," Mason said.

"May not what?"

"Ask that question," Mason said.

The editor laughed. "All right; you've aroused my interest and you've certainly injected an element of mystery into this. We had a lead that would have, I think, paid off. Ellen Calvert's mother married Henry Leland Berry, and we can check the residence in the marriage license and . . ."

"And work yourself into a sizable lawsuit," Mason said. "I don't want to argue with you. I don't want to intimidate you."

"Well, I'm not easily intimidated."

"That's fine," Mason said. "Have your lawyer get in touch with me on the telephone. The name is Perry Mason, and . . ."

"You don't need to tell me a second time," the editor said. "You're not entirely unknown, Mr. Mason. Many of your cases have been featured in the wire services. We've even published some of your spectacular courtroom cross-examinations."

"All right," Mason said, "let your attorney talk with me."

The editor said, "Forget it; the story is killed. Thank you for calling, Mr. Mason."

"O.K.," Mason said. "Good-bye."

Mason hung up, turned to his client. "The story is killed."

"Mr. Mason," she said, "I'm eternally grateful."

She opened her purse, handed him a fifty-dollar bill.

Mason said to Della Street, "Get her address, Della; give her back thirty dollars with a receipt for twenty dollars as a retainer and for services rendered to date. I don't think you'll have any more trouble, Miss Adair. If you do, get in touch with me."

"Thank you very much," she said, "but I cannot leave any address." She arose with queenly dignity and gave Mason her hand.

"We should be able to reach you in case of complications," Mason said.

The woman shook her head with quiet finality. "No address," she said.

"I'm sorry," Mason told her. "I won't try to reach you unless your own best interests require it, but I'll have to have a phone number or something."

Ellen Adair hesitated, then picked up a scratch pad, scribbled a telephone number, handed it to Della Street.

"Don't let *anyone* know that number," she said. "Don't try to call me except in a real emergency."

"We'll be highly discreet," Mason promised.

Ellen Adair took the receipt and the change Della Street gave her, included both Mason and Della Street in a gracious smile, and started for the door to the outer office.

"You can go out this way," Mason said, indicating the corridor door of the private office.

Della Street held the door open.

"Thank you," Ellen Adair said, and made a dignified exit.

When the door had closed, Mason glanced quizzically

at Della Street. "Now there, Della," he said, "is a story."

"How much of a story?"

"We don't know," Mason said, "but the situation is like an iceberg: only a small fraction of it shows above the water.

"Here's a girl who wins a beauty contest, who thinks she has the world at her feet, when suddenly she discovers she's pregnant. That was twenty years ago, when people simply didn't do those things and get away with them. Many a young woman committed suicide rather than face the so-called shame.

"Here was a young woman who took things in her stride, who held her chin up, who severed all connections with her friends and relatives and stood on her own two feet and developed a certain queenly air about her. She wouldn't knuckle under to anyone."

"On the other hand," Della Street said, "she never dared to get married. She probably felt she couldn't marry without telling her prospective husband—and there, again, times have changed."

Mason nodded thoughtfully. "I wonder," he said, "what became of the baby."

"It would be nineteen years old now," Della Street said, "and . . . Chief, what do you suppose *did* become of the baby? That's a story in itself."

"She didn't want us to ask that question," Mason said, "so I didn't ask it. She wanted the story killed. We've killed it."

The lawyer looked at his watch and said, "And it's just about time for my next appointment. The life of a lawyer is just one damn thing after another."

Chapter Two

It was two o'clock the next afternoon when Della Street, answering a call from the receptionist, said into the telephone, "Just a moment; I'll call you back, Gertie."

Della dropped the telephone into its cradle, said to Perry Mason, "We have a man in the outer office who says his business is urgent. His name is Jarmen Dayton. He says that he has to see you right away upon a matter of the greatest importance—to you.

"Gertie told him he would have to have more specific information than that and he said he was representing *The Cloverville Gazette*."

"An attorney?" Mason asked.

"Apparently not," she said. "He gave Gertie only the name of Jarmen Dayton."

The lawyer's eyes narrowed. "I had a hunch about that case yesterday," he said. "Bring Dayton in, Della, and we'll find out exactly what he wants."

Della nodded, left the office, and returned with a man

in his late forties. He was partially bald and of stout build, and he affected a brusque manner.

"Mr. Mason!" he exclaimed, pushing his way across the office, holding out a rather pudgy, short-fingered hand. "This is indeed a pleasure! A very great pleasure!"

The lawyer shook hands.

"I've come quite a distance to see you, sir. I thought perhaps I'd have some trouble since I had no appointment, but . . ."

"You *could* have telephoned," Mason said.

"Believe it or not, Mr. Mason, I've been going too fast to pause for telephones, had to catch a jet plane by the skin of my eyeteeth—just barely did make it.

"Don't like to run; doctor told me not to. But in an emergency you forget about everything except catching that plane. Mind if I sit down?"

"Please do," Mason said. "Now you're representing *The Cloverville Gazette?*"

"That's right. Thought I'd better come out here and have a talk with you."

"You're an attorney?"

The man ran a hand over his high forehead, brought his palm down along the back of his neck, then rubbed the side of his jaw. "Not exactly," he said.

"Well, let's be exact," Mason said; "either you are or you aren't."

"I'm not."

"You're an employee of the paper?"

"Well, there again I have to say not exactly. Now, don't start cross-examining me, Mason. I know the managing editor quite well, and he thought I'd better talk with you man to man—no telephone stuff, you understand, just right across the desk, eyeball to eyeball, face to face, man to man, put our cards right on the table."

Mason tapped the blotter on his desk with his forefinger. "There's the table."

"This Calvert case," Dayton said. "Something of a mystery there—and a story, a whale of a story. Now, of course, the paper doesn't want any lawsuits, but the paper *does* want the story. The darn thing is twenty years old, but people still talk about it—that is, the old-timers—garbled versions, all that sort of thing—not fair to the community, not fair to Ellen Calvert."

"Let's get this straight," Mason said. "The newspaper sent you all the way out here to talk with me and try to get that Calvert story—and all the newspaper wants it for is to put an item in its column of what happened twenty years ago. Is that right?"

Again Dayton rubbed his hand over his head. "Well, now, Mr. Mason," he said, "you keep putting me in a spot —you really do. The truth of the matter is that after the newspaper published this little lead that was sent in by one of its readers asking what had happened to Ellen Calvert, the phone started ringing. Readers in droves rang up and said that they had always wondered about Ellen Calvert, that it was a story the paper should publish.

"Now the paper may have been just a little conservative when you talked with the editor yesterday. Of course, you understand time is a couple of hours later back there.

Anyway, when they got to checking things—well, it was thought I'd better come out here and put the cards on the table."

"Keep putting them on the table," Mason said, "and turn them face up."

"Well, we want to find her. We want to find out what's happened to her. We're even in a position to make a payment—a very substantial payment."

"For a country newspaper?" Mason asked.

"We aren't country any more," Dayton said; "we're city."

"How much?" Mason asked.

Dayton's eyes studied Mason's face. "A payment to you, Counselor, for your cooperation and a payment for Ellen Calvert."

"How much?"

"How much would be required?"

"I don't know."

"I think," Dayton said, "we could put up the required amount, whatever it might be—that is, of course, within reason, you understand, Mr. Mason, within reason."

"I'll have to give that matter some consideration," Mason said.

"Of course you will, Mr. Mason, of course, of course. You'll have to take it up with your client. I understand perfectly."

Dayton abruptly got to his feet. "Do you want to call me or shall I call you?"

"You had better give me a number where I can reach you," the lawyer said.

"I'll have to call you a little later and give you the number, Mr. Mason. I have been traveling all night, you understand. I came to your office right away. I haven't had a chance to get a hotel room or get freshened up. I wanted to see you at once—I anticipated I might have some delays—I know you're a busy man—very prominent lawyer —more than that, a famous lawyer. I'll be in touch with you. Thank you for seeing me. Good day, Mr. Mason."

Dayton didn't even turn toward the room from which he had entered but marched directly to the door leading to the outer corridor and went out.

"A private detective," Mason said to Della Street; "one of the tough boys who carries a gun. He gets results by stopping at nothing. You have our client's telephone number?"

She nodded.

"All right," Mason said, "we'll call her shortly; but first get the Drake Detective Agency on the line. Get Paul Drake in person if you can, Della."

Della put through the call to the Drake Detective Agency, whose offices were next to the elevator at the end of the corridor, on the same floor as the lawyer's office.

When Mason had Paul Drake on the line, he said, "Paul, I have just been interviewed by a man who is undoubtedly a private detective. He is too portly to conceal the bulge under his left armpit. He's a tough customer. He was sent here from the Midwest to locate a client of mine. He thinks I am going to get in touch with that client either by telephone or personally, and since it is a matter I would hardly take up over the telephone, I think I may be wearing a tail.

"Now, here's what I'm going to do. In precisely

ten minutes from the time I hang up the telephone I am
going to go to the elevator. I want you to get aboard the
same elevator and ride down with me. Just speak to me
casually.

"We'll ride down together, then separate, and I'll walk
to the taxi stand on the corner, pick up a cab, and go to
the railroad depot. Once there, I'll go into a telephone
booth, put through a call, walk out, get another cab, and
come back to the office. I want you to have an operative
waiting in a cab so I can be tailed to see if I am being shadowed by anyone else.

"Can you do that?"

"Can do," Drake said. "I've got a couple of operatives
in the office right now, making out some reports. I can
send one of them down and have him engage a cab and
be waiting."

"Do that," Mason said; "if he should lose me at a traffic signal, you can tell him to drive right to the depot and
pick up my trail there. I'll wait around the telephone
booths for a minute or two before putting in the call.
Look at your watch now; we're going out in exactly ten
minutes."

Mason hung up the phone, said to Della, "Give me
Ellen Adair's telephone number, Della."

Della Street, watching him curiously, said, "Aren't you
going to a lot of trouble and a lot of expense just on mere
suspicion?"

"It's not mere suspicion," Mason said. "If that man
wasn't a private detective, I'll go see my oculist. And when
a small city newspaper sends a private detective instead
of a reporter to get a story, it means something big is in

the wind. Furthermore, I have a hunch there are two men on the job. One of them may be local, but this one came from Cloverville."

Promptly at the end of nine minutes and forty-five seconds, Mason left his office, walked to the elevator, and pressed the down button.

Just before the cage came to a stop, Paul Drake emerged from his office.

"Hi, Perry," Drake said; "what's new?"

"Nothing much," Mason said.

"You aren't quitting for the day?"

"Heavens, no! Just have to consult with a client on a matter of business."

They entered the cage together.

"Going to see a client, eh?" Drake asked.

"Uh-huh," Mason said, without making any effort to carry on further conversation.

In the foyer of the building, Drake paused to buy a package of cigarettes. Mason strolled across to the sidewalk, hailed a taxicab.

"Take me to the Union Depot," he instructed, and settled back against the cushions.

The driver skillfully threaded his way through traffic and duly deposited Mason at the station.

Mason paid the fare, gave the cabby a tip, and walked toward the line of telephone booths near the station entrance. He entered one and stood so that his shoulders concealed the dial of the telephone from anyone who might have been watching to see what number he dialed; then he dialed the number of Paul Drake's office.

Drake's switchboard operator came on the line and

Mason said, "Perry Mason, Ruth. Is Paul where you can put him on?"

"He's just receiving a telephone report from one of his operatives," she said. "I think it's on the case that you're interested in."

"I'll hang on," Mason said, and waited some two minutes at the telephone. Then he heard Paul Drake's voice.

"Hi, Perry; you're down at the telephone booths at the depot?"

"Right."

"Well, you're wearing a tail all right."

"A heavyset individual in the late forties with . . ."

"No, this is a thin older man about sixty with high cheekbones. He's wearing a dark-brown suit, black shoes, white shirt and brown tie. He seems to know his way around."

"I think probably he is local," Mason said. "What's a job like that worth, Paul?"

"If he's local, he's probably getting forty to fifty dollars a day and expenses," Drake said. "He was planted in a taxicab outside the building."

"Well," Mason said, "I've got a problem on my hands, Paul. I'm going to have to employ a decoy."

"What kind of a decoy?"

"A woman, about thirty-eight years old, quite tall—a little taller than the average—about five feet eight and a half. Light-chestnut hair, if possible. I want her to weigh a hundred and thirty to a hundred and thirty-two pounds. I want her to be quick on the uptake, and she'll need an apartment. She'll go under the name of Ellen Smith. She'll surround herself with an air of mystery, avoid contacts with anyone, and be in a position to follow instructions.

"I'd like to have her in an apartment if possible, but I don't want her to get an apartment which was leased just a few hours earlier if I can avoid it. I . . ."

"That end of it is all right," Drake said. "As part of the operation we keep a dummy, decoy apartment in the name of the switchboard operator, but the rent is handled in such a way that no one could ever trace the apartment to this office.

"It's going to take me a little while to make all the arrangements you want, but I have a list of female operators and one of them fits your description to a T. I don't think she's working now, and I'll try and get her.

"Now, Perry, there's one thing you've got to watch out for. If anybody has gone to all this trouble to sew you up, you had better be careful with your telephone conversations. With electronic eavesdropping devices it's not too difficult to bug an office or tap a telephone line."

Mason said, "That's why I'm telephoning you from the depot, Paul. I'll telephone you again shortly. See if your operative is available, and if she is I want her to come to my office in about half an hour. Can do?"

"If she's available, can do," Drake said. "You call me back in ten minutes."

"Right," Mason said.

The lawyer hung up, left the telephone booth, walked halfway to the entrance of the depot, then suddenly snapped his fingers as though he had forgotten something, whirled on his heel, and started back toward the telephone booths.

He almost collided with a rather thin individual with high cheekbones, a lantern jaw, a brown suit and tie, black shoes, and white shirt. The man was about sixty years of age.

Mason hurried back to the telephone booth, again held his body in such a position that his shoulders shielded the dial of the telephone, and dialed the number Ellen Adair had given Della Street.

A voice at the other end of the line repeated the number Mason had dialed.

"Miss Adair, please," Mason said.

"Just a moment, please," the voice said.

A few moments later another voice said, "Miss Adair's office."

"Miss Adair, please," Mason said.

"Who's calling?"

"Mr. Mason."

"Just a moment, please."

A moment later Mason heard Ellen Adair's voice.

"Listen carefully," Mason said. "I want to know where I stand. What kind of a game are you playing? Are you mixed up in a criminal case—and, if so, what are the facts?"

"What are you talking about?" Ellen Adair demanded.

"I'm talking about the fact that somebody from Cloverville showed up in my office and said that he was representing *The Cloverville Gazette,* that the story of what had happened to you was arousing a tremendous amount of local interest, that the paper would be willing to pay a reasonable sum for your story."

"Oh my God!" Ellen Adair exclaimed.

"Wait a minute: you haven't heard it all yet," Mason said. "I pegged this man as a private detective. I surmised that he would feel I might be getting in touch with you, that my phone might be tapped or my office bugged, so I took a cab to the depot. I'm calling you from the phone booth there. I was followed to the depot by another man, who may be a local private detective.

"Now all of this is costing somebody a lot of money. I think the one private detective really did come in from Cloverville. The other man who is on my tail seems to know the city pretty well and may well be a local man. Even so, someone has put a few hundred dollars on the line right up to date.

"Now then, if you're that important and you've mixed me into the case, I want to know why you're that important."

"I can't tell you," she said; "not now."

"I didn't think you could," Mason said, "but I want to know where I can meet you at seven-thirty tonight. I'll be accompanied by Della Street, and we'll have dinner and be where we can talk. We can get reasonable privacy at The Blue Ox. Do you ever eat there?"

"I'm familiar with it," she said. "Can I meet you there at seven-thirty and be sure that the people who are following you wouldn't—wouldn't pick me up?"

Mason said, "I think so. I think I can arrange it.

"Now look—all this cloak-and-dagger stuff makes me very, very suspicious. I am afraid that I am being dragged into something that . . ."

"No, no, no, Mr. Mason," she interrupted, "it's nothing that will affect you. It's only something that affects me, but I need you now more than ever. I know now who's back of all this and I simply must have your help. I'm prepared to pay whatever it's worth."

"All right," Mason said; "I'm going to play ball with you because I had an idea yesterday there was a lot more to the case than you were telling me. Also, I don't like to have some private detective try to make a monkey out of me.

"Now, correct me if I am wrong. These people—whoever they are—who are on your trail haven't seen you for some twenty years. They knew you as a good-looking girl —in fact, a beautiful girl—who was a little above the average height. Any rather tall woman who is good-looking and about the right age might be used as a decoy—is that right?"

"Yes."

"It's difficult for you to talk where you are now?"

"Yes."

"May I ask where that is?"

Ellen Adair said, "You are talking with the head buyer of French, Coleman and Swazey, and any understanding you have with me will be honored."

"Thank you," Mason said. "I'll see you at The Blue Ox at seven-thirty. Tell the headwaiter that you are Mr. Mason's guest and he'll show you to a booth."

The lawyer waited for several minutes, then again called Drake's office.

Paul Drake himself answered the phone.

"Perry?"

"Right."

"Everything's O.K. I've got the operative, and she'll move into the apartment with at least enough stuff to enable her to *act* as if she's living there. She'll probably have to eat out."

"When can she be at my office?"

"Any time you say within the next thirty to forty minutes."

Mason said, "Have her at my office in exactly forty minutes. Then I want her to leave a broad trail from the office right to the apartment. In other words, Paul, we're going to be naïve. We're going to play everything wide open. It will be so easy to follow her that it will be like rolling off a log. Only don't make it *too* simple. I don't want these people to suspect a frame-up, but I do want them to believe that they're dealing with an unsuspecting attorney who won't prove to be too formidable an adversary.

"Now, here's something else. Della Street and I are going to be at The Blue Ox Café tonight. I'll have a table reserved. I want to be absolutely certain that I am not followed, and if I should be followed I want to be tipped off so that I can take my shadow on a detour. Della and I will come in a taxicab. We'll be there on the dot at seven-thirty. I want you to have an operative on the job to make sure I'm not being followed. I don't think I will be, but I have to be absolutely certain.

"Got everything straight?"

"I have it all straight," Drake said. "Ellen Smith will be at your office in exactly forty minutes. She'll give the name 'Ellen Smith' to the receptionist and say she has an appointment. She'll talk with you, then leave and go directly to the decoy apartment and stay there until she receives further orders."

"That's right," Mason said. "Now, you've got some kind of a bug detector which can tell if an office is bugged?"

"That's right."

"Go in my office," Mason said, "and make sure that there are no bugs."

"I can't check your phone in that time," Drake said. "They've got so many methods of . . ."

"Forget the phone," Mason told him, "and I don't think you'll find any bugs in the office. They think I'm a pushover.

"I'll be in touch with you from time to time, giving you instructions. I can trust this Ellen Smith?"

"With your life," Drake said.

"O.K.," Mason told him, and hung up.

The lawyer left the station, took a cab directly back to his office, entered through the corridor door to his private office, turned to Della Street, and said, "What's new, Della?"

"Paul has been here with a bug detector and has given the office a clean bill of health," she said. "No bugs."

"That's fine," Mason told her. "I didn't think there'd be any."

"Can you tell me what this is all about?" Della asked.

"Not yet," Mason said, "but you have a dinner date with the boss and a client tonight, so prepare to wrap yourself around a nice, juicy steak with all the trimmings. Unless I'm greatly mistaken, we're going to be mixed up to our eyebrows in intrigue. A rather tall woman, thirty-eight years old, is going to be in the office within about ten minutes. I want to see her. She'll give the name of Ellen Smith. Tell Gertie she has an appointment and she's to come right in."

"And who, may I ask, is Ellen Smith?"

"Ellen Smith," Mason said, grinning, "is a ringer."

"A ringer?"

"That's right. A double for our client, Ellen Adair. When she leaves the office she's going to be followed to her apartment."

"And then?" Della Street asked.

Mason said, "Our friend Jarmen Dayton will, from that moment, be very difficult to deal with. We'll find that *The Cloverville Gazette* is very, very penny-pinching. The talk of generous compensation which we heard earlier today will fade away into the background. Our friend Mr. Dayton will wish us a very good day and leave us badly mystified."

"And what will you do?"

"Oh, I'll be badly mystified," Mason said, grinning. "You never want to disappoint a private detective who has spent the night on a jet plane and who hasn't had time even to go to a hotel and freshen up but who did have time to go to a local private detective agency and engage an operative to back up his play."

Della sighed. "If you didn't get such a kick out of cases of this sort, you'd get bored with it all. I suppose you're running up a big bill with Paul Drake's office, and so far we have no client to charge it to."

"I'm the client in this particular transaction," Mason said. "I'm trying to find out why a young woman who had won a beauty contest and thought she had the world at her feet would become pregnant and disappear, remain unmarried for twenty years, then hire an attorney to keep a local newspaper from publishing an item in the column entitled 'Cloverville's Yesterdays.' "

"And what," Della Street asked, "became of the baby?"

"I think," Mason told her, "that when we start asking questions about that, we'll find our client will tell us to go fly a kite."

"Why?" Della Street asked.

"If we knew the answer to that," Mason said, "we'd probably know why *The Cloverville Gazette* sent a private detective out here and why someone is paying to have me shadowed."

Mason, feeling in a particularly happy mood, brought out the coffee percolator and said, "I think that entitles us to a coffee break, Della."

They had only started drinking their coffee when the telephone rang and Gertie said, "Ellen Smith is here."

"Tell her to come in," Mason said. "Wait a minute. Della will come out and get her."

Della Street went to the outer office and, a few moments later, came back with a woman who was almost exactly the same height and build as Ellen Adair.

Mason looked her over approvingly.

"Credentials?" he asked.

She opened her purse and showed him her credentials as one of Drake's operatives.

"We have to be cautious in a deal of this sort," Mason said. "Sit down. We've got about ten or fifteen minutes to kill, and I take it you could perhaps use a cup of coffee."

"I'd love it."

"Do you mind telling me your exact age?" Mason asked.

"Thirty-two to prospective employers, thirty to prospective swains, and thirty-eight when accuracy is essential."

Mason grinned. "I think you have what it takes."

Della handed the woman a cup of coffee.

Then the woman said, "Would you mind telling me what this is all about?"

"Frankly," Mason said, "we don't know. I am going to tell you this much about which I am certain.

"Since you will take the name of Ellen Smith for the purpose of this job, we are going to call you Ellen Smith and not your true name.

"You are taking the name of Ellen Smith because people are going to mistake you for an Ellen Calvert who at one time lived in the Midwest in a rural city which has since grown considerably.

"You—as Ellen Calvert—left that city twenty years ago under mysterious circumstances, and certain people are trying to find out what those circumstances were, where you have been, and what happened to you.

"I *think* that there are a lot of other things which these people are trying to find out, but I'm not prepared to say what they are.

"The reason you are here is that I was approached a short time ago by a man who put me in such a position that he felt certain I would telephone my client—who, incidentally, is the real Ellen Calvert—and ask her to come in to discuss a proposition which he had made.

"I know that I have been shadowed and I have every reason to believe the office is being kept under surveillance. Because you are about the same build and age as the real Ellen Calvert, when you leave this office you will be shadowed.

"Now, as I understand it, the Drake Detective Agency has an apartment which they use from time to time."

"That's right. Mr. Drake keeps people there when he has some witness whom he doesn't dare to register in a local hotel. It's also a place where operatives can take a potential witness when they want to get a statement. The place is bugged and a tape recorder takes down things that are said.

"It's not a particularly large or expensive apartment. It's just a utility place."

"I think it will do," Mason said. "When you leave here you're to take a taxi and go to that apartment. It has a back door?"

"Front and back, yes. There's a service entrance in the back."

Mason said, "Once you have been shadowed to that apartment, once you produce a key and go inside as though you owned the place, there will be a period of an hour or so when you will be free.

"I feel that you will be shadowed as far as the apartment, then the detective who shadows you will leave to make a report to his agency. Having run you to earth, so to speak, they will do nothing more for an hour or two, or perhaps a day or two, while they await instructions.

"Now then, as soon as you have entered the apartment with a latchkey, go right through the apartment. Slip out the back door. That opens on an alley?"

"Yes."

"Drake will have an operative waiting with a car to pick you up. You can go to your own apartment, pack up suitcases with whatever you will need for a stay of several days.

"Since I can't get you bona fide employment which would stand up under scrutiny, you are going to have to take the part of a young woman who is temporarily out of a job. You will live economically. You will go to the cheaper family restaurants and you will buy provisions at the supermarket."

"There's one within a block and a half of the place," she said.

Mason nodded. "You will use taxicabs when you have to, but as sparingly as possible. I don't dare have you use one of Drake's automobiles because they could and would trace the license number.

"I think that sooner or later someone will come to the door and start talking with you. No matter what the approach is, no matter how plausible it may seem, you are to slam the door in his face.

"He may be offering you an opportunity to enroll in a contest where there will be prizes. He may be selling lottery tickets. He may come right out and accuse you of being Ellen Calvert and tell you that there's no use trying to keep up the pretense, that your story is known to him.

He may simply offer you money for your story. He may come right out and tell you he is a private detective, that he wants certain facts and that it will be easier for you to give him those facts than for him to have to get them the hard way."

"No matter what the approach is, I'm to slam the door in his face?"

"Yes."

"Do I deny that I am Ellen Calvert?"

"You are tight-lipped," Mason said. "You simply slam the door. The apartment has a telephone?"

"Yes."

"Do you know the number?"

"Paul Drake has it."

"I'll get it from Paul," Mason said.

"Anything else?"

"When you leave here," Mason said, "you are to be very much disturbed, yet with it all you have a queenly dignity. Keep your head up, but show that you are emotionally upset. You wipe an imaginary tear from your eye. You twist your handkerchief. Halfway to the elevator, you pause as though you had thought of something important. You turn around and take two or three steps back toward the office, then shrug your shoulders, apparently change your mind, go back to the elevator. . . . Now, of course, you're familiar with this apartment?"

"I've used it several times. I had a female witness to keep under cover."

"It would be better," Mason said, "if you know the exact route, to go there by bus rather than by taxicab."

"That's easy," she said, smiling. "Not all of our clients

are sufficiently affluent to afford cab bills for operatives and I've gone there half-a-dozen times by bus."

"It's highly important that you don't make any mistakes on that," Mason said. "If you get on the wrong bus, it would be a dead giveway. You'll probably be followed from the minute you leave the office, and it will make it much easier if you give your shadow an opportunity to get aboard the same bus with you."

She nodded. "I think I've got the picture."

"Under no circumstances," Mason said, "at any time are you to use the name of Ellen Calvert or to admit that you are Ellen Calvert. If anybody presses you for a name, you say that you are Ellen Smith. The main thing is to keep the door closed whenever anyone tries to interrogate you, but you will do it under circumstances which indicate you definitely have something to conceal."

"Am I supposed to be an embezzler or something?" she asked.

Mason shook his head. "You're just supposed to be a woman who is trying to avoid her past."

She smiled. "I must have quite a purple past," she said, "if I haven't been guilty of any crime."

Mason nodded gravely. "That," he said, "is something that I am also keeping in mind."

She finished her coffee, handed the cup to Della Street, and said, "Could I have just another half cup, please?"

While Della poured the coffee, the operative sized up Mason. "I've heard a lot about you," she said. "This is the first time I've ever worked directly on one of your cases. I think I'm going to enjoy it."

"I certainly hope so," Mason said. "Unless things come

to a head rather promptly, it's going to be rather tedious
for you, sitting there in an apartment and . . ."

"Oh, there's a television and a radio," she said. "I'll
pick up a couple of books that I've been trying to read and
I'll get along fine. This is a vacation with pay as far as I'm
concerned. You should see some of the jobs I get mixed
up with."

"I guess it's an adventurous life," Mason said.

"You can say that again," she observed.

She placed the cup and saucer on the edge of the filing
case. "Ready for me to go?" she asked.

"O.K.," Mason said. "I'll get the number of the
telephone from Paul Drake. You have my number. You
can call me if anything turns up, but remember that both
lines may be tapped after you have been there for a day or
so. It will take them a day to concentrate on getting some
electronic device in operation. Just be careful—and, above
all, be just Ellen. Don't use your last name when you call
me. Say, 'This is Ellen speaking.' "

"I've got it," she said.

Mason moved over to the exit door. "Remember now,"
he cautioned, "be naïve. Stand tall, be dignified. Act natural, but be entirely unsuspecting."

"Will do," she said, flashed him a smile, and moved out
of the office, holding her chin high.

Mason returned and held out his coffee cup to Della
Street.

"Well?" she asked.

Mason grinned. "To hell with all the routine stuff,
Della. This is the sort of thing which makes a lawyer's
life worthwhile."

"To whom are you going to charge all these expenses?" she asked.

Mason grinned. "So far, to me. This is as good as a vacation."

"Some holiday!" she said.

Mason put a powdered cream substitute and sugar in his coffee, stirred the liquid thoughtfully. "We will take the utmost precautions to see that we're not followed tonight, Della," he announced, "but I think that our decoy will be working. I think we'll have sent the hounds baying off on a false scent."

"You," Della Street charged, "are as happy as a kid with a new toy."

"I am for a fact," Mason agreed.

Chapter Three

MASON AND DELLA STREET entered The Blue Ox promptly at seven-thirty. The headwaiter came forward deferentially. "Your booth is ready, Mr. Mason, and you have someone waiting."

"Has that someone been here long?" Mason asked.

"About five minutes."

"Description?"

"Rather tall woman with a commanding presence, somewhere in her early thirties or perhaps her late twenties . . ."

Della Street winked at Perry Mason.

"Ever the diplomat," Mason said. "I'll be sure to tell her. All right, lead the way, Pierre."

The headwaiter ushered them to Mason's booth. As he pulled aside the curtain, Ellen Adair looked up apprehensively, and her face showed relief as she saw Mason and Della Street.

"You're a little early," Mason said.

She nodded.

"Cocktail?" Mason asked.

"A dry Martini, please."

"Two Bacardis and a dry Martini," Mason said to Pierre. "Will you see that we get them, Pierre?"

"Right away."

"Hungry?" Mason asked.

"Not particularly."

"Now then," Mason said, "keep your voice low and tell me what this is all about."

"Mr. Mason," she said, "I have some money. I am not wealthy. I have the money which came to me from my mother's estate, and I have some savings. I am the head buyer at French, Coleman and Swazey, and for reasons which I can't go into I simply can't afford to have my identity disclosed. That is, I can't afford to be discovered as Ellen Calvert."

"Can you tell me why?"

She hesitated a moment, then slowly shook her head.

"These people from Cloverville, or this one person, at least," Mason said, "do you know him? Do you have any ideas? Pudgy, forty-five, partially bald, with . . ."

She shook her head before Mason had finished the description.

A waitress brought their cocktails.

"Give us ten minutes," Mason said, "and then bring us another round and the menu, please."

The waitress nodded and withdrew.

"You won a beauty contest and you were pregnant," Mason said.

"Yes."

"Pregnancy requires two people. Who was the other person?"

"Do you have to know?"

"If I'm going to help you, I do."

She sipped her cocktail thoughtfully, then said, "I was eighteen. I was good-looking. People said I was beautiful. I thought the world was my oyster. The man in the case was about five years older. He was the son of a very wealthy man, a . . . a social big shot. I was flattered by his attention. I was also in love."

"Was he in love?" Mason asked.

She hesitated, then looked Mason in the eyes and said, "I don't know. At the time I thought not."

"Why do you say that?" Mason asked.

She said, "I was looking forward to a career. I had everything. Then, all of a sudden, the whole structure collapsed. I found I was pregnant.

"Remember this was twenty years ago, Mr. Mason. When I realized the situation, I went into a complete panic."

"You got in touch with your boyfriend?"

"At once."

"And what did he do?"

"He was just as frightened as I was, but his father was president of a big company. My boyfriend told me not to worry, that they had a man whose duty it was to build public relations to give the company a good image. He said that person would know how I could get fixed up."

"And you?"

"I told him I didn't want that—that I couldn't go to

an abortionist. He asked me if I was old-fashioned or something, and we left each other with a feeling of mutual irritation. He couldn't see my position; I couldn't see his."

"And what happened?"

"This expert in the field of public relations knew what to do all right," she said. "The next day I received an envelope by special messenger. There was no return address on the envelope. I opened it, and there were ten hundred-dollar bills in it. The next day I read in the paper that my boyfriend had left that afternoon on an extensive European trip. I never saw him again."

"Where is he now?"

"I don't know."

Mason toyed with the stem of his cocktail glass. "I think you do," he said.

"Well," she admitted after a few moments, "I know this much: about a year after he returned from Europe he married a young woman whom he had met on the trip. The marriage was not particularly happy from all I can learn, but they stayed together."

"What happened to her?" Mason asked.

"She died about a year and a half ago."

"Any children?"

"No."

"What about the boy's father?"

"His father died ten years ago, and the son inherited the company."

Mason said, "Has it occurred to you that this letter to *The Cloverville Gazette* suggesting that you would make

a very fine subject for a story in 'Cloverville's Yesterdays' was not just accidental but was part of a well-laid
plan to locate you?"

"Has it occurred to you?" she countered.

"In the light of subsequent developments I think it is a
logical explanation," Mason said.

"All right," she admitted, "it occurred to me. It occurred to me as soon as I saw the column. It occurred to
me when I had a blind panic. It occurred to me when I
went to your office to enlist your aid."

"Any idea who it might be?" Mason asked.

The shake of her head was too emphatic and too instantaneous.

Mason smiled. "You are a little *too* emphatic in your
denial, Ellen. How about the man who is the father of
your child?"

"I haven't said anything about a child."

"You have very carefully avoided saying anything
about a child," Mason said. "But you admit you went in a
blind panic. You were opposed to abortion. A logical explanation is that you had a child, that that child must be
nineteen years old at the moment.

"You have made your mistakes; you have lived them
down; you have established yourself in a new position of
responsibility; you have a career.

"Times have changed. The fact that you may have had
an illegitimate child nineteen years ago means little today. It would, of course, cause a few uplifted eyebrows,
but nothing to get panicky about.

"Therefore," Mason said, "I conclude that your panic
is because of something concerning this child."

"You are too . . . too damned logical," she said.

"And correct?"

She hesitated a moment, then met his eyes. "And correct. I am going to protect him . . . my child."

"It was a boy, then," Mason said.

"Very well; it's a son, and I am going to protect him."

"From what?"

"From his father."

"A boy is entitled to a father," Mason said.

"During the formative years he's entitled to a father whom he can look up to and respect—not a heel who runs off to Europe and leaves a pregnant sweetheart behind to face the music by herself."

"And more than that?" Mason asked.

"I can't tell him," she said. "I have to protect him."

"From the knowledge that he is illegitimate?"

"Partially that."

"I think," Mason said, "you'd better tell me the truth."

The waitress brought the second round of cocktails and the menus. They ordered three steaks. The waitress withdrew.

Ellen Adair picked up her cocktail glass, drained a good half of it. "Don't try to corner me," she said.

"I'm simply trying to get the information I'm going to need so that I can help you," Mason told her.

"All right," she said; "I'll tell you this much: I was a young, foolish, unsophisticated, good-looking girl. I was pregnant. I had a thousand dollars. That was every cent I had to my name. I know now what the public-relations man or troubleshooter or whatever you want to call him had in mind. He thought that I would use some of the money to go away from home and then use the rest of it for an abortion, then return to my parents with some story about having been emotionally disturbed and . . ."

"But you didn't do that," Mason said.

"I didn't do that," she said. "I came out here and got a job."

"What kind of a job?"

"Doing housework."

"And what happened?"

"It wasn't long before the woman I was working for, who was very shrewd and rather suspicious, found out I was pregnant.

"She and her husband were childless. They had been trying to adopt a baby. They couldn't adopt one because of personal reasons that had nothing to do with their competency as parents.

"The woman suggested that we move to San Francisco, that when it came time for the baby to arrive I go to the hospital and take her name, that the birth certificate would show the child as hers. They promised to treat him as their own child. They were nice people."

"That was done?" Mason asked.

"That was done."

"The boy thinks those people are his parents?"

"Yes."

"Does he know you?"

She tossed off the last of her cocktail. "That, Mr. Mason, is something that is none of your business. I have told you enough so you can understand my position, so you can realize that I want protection. I am in a position to pay your fee.

"All I can say is that those people must never, never, never find me."

"You mean never, never, never find your son?"

"It's the same thing."

"The boy's real father," Mason said, "inherited a rather large company when his father died?"

"I suppose so, yes."

"And, by the same token, is now rather wealthy?"

"I suppose so."

"He would be in a position to give your boy a first-class education?"

"He could probably be made to support him and educate him in accordance with his style of life, but my son is now nineteen years old and any advantage he could get would be far outweighed by corresponding disadvantages."

"But," Mason said, "suppose the boy's father should die?"

"All right," she said; "with that lawyer mind of yours you've probably put your finger on the sore spot."

"Which is?" Mason asked.

"That the boy's real father is now single and childless, that he has two half brothers who have no interest whatever in the manufacturing plant. If the man in question should die without a will, and without children, they would be in a position to inherit. If there was a child, even an illegitimate child, who could show up, the situation would be different. If the man in the case should leave a will stating that he has reason to believe that somewhere he has a son or a daughter, that the bulk of his property is to go to that son or daughter—well, the half brothers would be out of luck."

"What kind of people are they?" Mason asked.

"Do you have to ask that question? Can't you see what is happening?" She pushed aside her cocktail glass. "And that's all the information you're going to get, Mr. Mason. It is your job to build a fence around me, to keep me concealed. Get a substitute, do anything you have to. Let the boy's father feel that his son is dead."

Mason slowly shook his head.

"Why not?"

"Your boy has rights."

"I'm his mother."

"And the man in the case is his father," Mason said.

"Unworthy to be his father."

"Unworthy or not," Mason said, "the father has rights. And the boy has rights too. Now I'll go this far with you: I'll try to keep them from finding you, at least for the moment. But I'm not going to do anything of which my conscience wouldn't approve."

"I don't think I want you on that basis," she said.

"You don't have to have me," Mason told her. "You have given me twenty dollars. That pays you up in full of account to date. If you want to get some other attorney, you are at liberty to do so."

"But you've been to a lot of expense. You've hired detectives and . . ."

"That," Mason said, "will be my contribution to the cause."

She hesitated a moment, then suddenly pushed back her chair. "As an attorney, Mr. Mason, you have to respect my confidence. You can't divulge any of the information I have given you. I don't know how much money you have spent on detectives, but here are two one-hundred-dollar bills. You may consider that you have withdrawn from the case or that the case has been withdrawn from you. The more I see of you, the more I think you will be too damned conscientious, and there are factors involved which you know nothing about.

"I am no longer hungry. I'll leave it to you to exercise the masculine prerogative of picking up the check.

"Good night." Her chin held high, she swept out of the booth.

Mason looked at the two one-hundred-dollar bills she had left on the table, looked ruefully at Della Street. "Is there a cat in your apartment building?" he asked. "A cat or a dog?"

"The people next door have a cat."

"When the waitress brings Ellen Adair's steak," Mason said, "we'll ask her to bring a Bowser bag. You can tell the cat that it's an ill wind that blows no one good."

Chapter Four

PROMPTLY at nine o'clock the next morning Paul Drake's code knock sounded on the door of Mason's private office.

Della Street let Drake in.

Paul Drake, tall, loose-jointed, casual in appearance, jackknifed himself into the client's overstuffed chair, interlaced the fingers of his hands over his right knee, grinned at Mason, and said, "Up to your neck again?"

"Up to my neck," Mason said.

"Hang it," Drake said, "if someone came in and asked you to draw up a chattel mortgage, you'd manage to make a first-class mystery out of it somewhere along the line and probably have a murder case out of it before you got done."

"What's happening now?" Mason asked.

"Well, of course," Drake said, "I don't want to inquire into your business, and there are certain things which very definitely are none of my affair, but you certainly have stirred up a mess."

"How come?"

"This decoy you hired yesterday—the tall girl."

"What about her?"

"She certainly proved a beautiful red herring and sent the pack baying off on a false scent."

"How big a pack?" Mason asked.

"Well," Drake said, "you got me interested in the case, Perry. I had to take a gander myself. The people who are on the job are pretty smooth workers, but they left a chink in their armor at that."

"Go on," Mason said.

"You may have noticed," Drake said, "that rental automobiles have different colors on the rearview mirrors."

"Colored mirrors?" Mason asked.

"The backs of the mirrors," Drake said. "The rearview mirror is over the windshield. When you look at it from the driver's position you see to the rear, but when you look at it from the front you see the metallic back of the mirror. Now the different rental companies color these mirrors in different colors so that anyone seeing the car approaching can tell that it's a rental car and, by the color, tell what company rented it."

Mason nodded. "I knew that, Paul. What about it?"

"Well," Drake said, "your decoy certainly did a job. She left the office and was tailed by your heavyset, baldish individual around forty-five. Then after she got to the street another man was waiting—this rather tall fellow with high cheekbones—a guy somewhere near sixty, thin and somber-looking."

"Go on," Mason said; "you interest me."

"Well, my operative took a bus out to the apartment.

Incidentally, Perry, here's the address of the apartment and the telephone number."

Drake handed across two cards. "One for you and one for Della," he said. "Slip this card in your pocket, Perry; you may want to call the number. I think you're going to have developments in the case."

"Why?" Mason asked.

"It's too hot," Drake said. "It's going to come to a boil."

"Go on, Paul."

"Well," the detective resumed, "after my operative got to the apartment she telephoned me that everything was okeydokey, that she had gone to the apartment, that a car had tailed her, that she'd followed your instructions and slipped out the back door, gone to her own apartment, packed up what clothes she needed for a four- or five-day stay, gone to the supermarket, loaded up with provisions, and then gone back to the hideout apartment and holed up.

"She said she hadn't been there over a couple of hours when two cars drove up. One driver was a man about forty-five, rather heavyset—in short, a man who answered to the description of your friend whom you felt was a detective. The other one was this tall, thin, somber-looking guy who, she said, looked like a reincarnated turkey buzzard. They parked their cars on opposite sides of the street, facing in opposite directions.

"Now that's a trick that you use only when you're really spending money on a shadowing job and can't afford to lose the subject or can't afford to lose anyone who comes to call on the subject. In other words, you have an automobile facing in each direction and either can take up a shadowing job without making a U-turn or doing anything that's conspicuous."

Mason nodded.

"Well," Drake said, "I thought I'd go out and take a look at the situation just to check on it and pick up the license numbers on these cars.

"As soon as I drove past the first car I saw the color of the mirror and knew it was a car from a drive-yourself agency, so I went down the street a few blocks and turned around and came back and checked on the mirror of the other car. They were both from the same agency.

"So I went to the agency, used a little pull, and checked on any persons from the Midwest who had been renting automobiles.

"As you know, these drive-yourself agencies insist on knowing the person with whom they're doing business and knowing that the person is a duly licensed driver. You have to show your automobile license in order to rent a car."

"Go on," Mason said.

Drake said, "Well, I got two names for you. Your heavyset man is Jarmen Dayton. He's from Cloverville. And the tall, cadaverous individual is Stephen Lockley Garland, also of Cloverville.

"So," Drake said, "I ran through my files and found that I have a real good contact in a city only twenty-five miles from Cloverville, so I gave my correspondent a ring and asked him if he knew a detective by the name of Jarmen Dayton. He did. Dayton follows a pattern. He was on the police force at Cloverville, worked up to be chief of police, got mixed up in a political hassle, got fired, opened up a private detective agency.

"So then we come to this man Garland—Stephen Lockley Garland. Now there's a guy."

"What about him?" Mason asked.

"The big thing in Cloverville is the Cloverville Spring and Suspension Company. It's an old firm. It's been in the same family for a generation or two and it owns the town. It's big: you don't get anywhere in Cloverville unless you kowtow to the Spring Company."

"Go on," Mason said.

"Well, this fellow Garland has been with the company for years. Ostensibly he's a public-relations man. Actually he's a troubleshooter, a fixer, and all the rest of it.

"If you're running for office in Cloverville, you hunt up Garland and make him a lot of campaign promises about what you'll do if you're elected. If you don't do that, you don't get elected.

"If something happens and someone does something the Spring Company doesn't approve of, Garland pussyfoots around to the city trustees, and the first thing you know there's an ordinance covering the situation. They have a nickname for him: they call him Slick Garland."

Mason grinned. "Looks like we've got the big guns trained on us, Paul."

"One other thing: my contact says the whole place is buzzing over the news that the head of the Cloverville Spring and Suspension Company has been lost at sea.

"His name's Harmon Haslett, and about two weeks ago he went off for a yachting trip in Europe. Somewhere in the Bay of Biscay they picked up distress signals from the yacht during a storm. The signals abruptly ceased. Several vessels went to the location given in the signals and found no trace of the yacht except a life preserver with the name of the yacht on it. The assumption is that the yacht went down with all on board.

"How strong do you want to go on this, Perry?"

"I'm damned if I know, Paul. I've been fired with two hundred dollars for expense money."

"Oh, oh," Drake said. "Even if I trimmed costs to the bone, you couldn't go very much farther on two hundred expenses. I didn't know you were working on such a tight margin."

"I didn't either," Mason said, "and I wasn't until I spoke out of turn. My client gave me a couple of hundred, and I'll just toss a couple of hundred into the kitty, Paul, because I'm curious."

"What do you want done?"

"For one thing, Paul, I'd like to find out if Harmon Haslett is the sole owner of the Cloverville Spring and Suspension company. I think he's the son of the founder. The father has probably died or retired. I'd like a little background on this guy.

"And, of course, I'd like to find out a little more about these people who are shadowing our decoy. I'd like to find out where they are staying and whether they have any local connections. I figured this man Garland as a local detective."

"Why?"

"He seemed to know his way around," Mason said.

"I think he knows his way around every big city in the

United States," Drake said. "The guy has fellows working for him, and evidently he has a pretty big job. He's a combined lobbyist, private detective, gumshoe artist, fixer and troubleshooter."

Mason grinned. "Let me know when your bill totals four hundred dollars, Paul."

"We stop there?" Drake asked.

Mason grinned. "How do I know?" he said. "This is interesting the hell out of me. Let's call it a vacation."

Drake nodded, said, "I'll keep you posted, Perry," and left the office.

"Get those names?" Mason asked Della Street.

Della, who had been taking notes of the conversation, nodded. "Want me to type them up?"

"No," Mason said, "I'll remember them. Jarmen Dayton, whom we already know, and Stephen Lockley Garland. This man Garland must be a character."

"You," she charged, "are going to put me in an impossible situation."

"How come?"

"How can I explain this added two hundred dollars to the Internal Revenue Service? They'll want to know what case it was on and where the money came from."

Mason grinned at her. "Tell them it's a lawyer's vacation," he said.

Della Street sighed. "At times you can show a great lack of sympathy for a person with secretarial responsibilities."

Chapter Five

It was midafternoon when Paul Drake again gave his code knock on Mason's door and Della Street let him in.

"Well, Perry," Drake said, "I've had more reports from Cloverville and I can give you the picture. I don't know what it's all about, but the information I have can be used by you to fill in the missing parts."

"Shoot," Mason said.

"The Cloverville Spring and Suspension Company is virtually a one-man concern. It was operated by Harmon Haslett until his death a few days ago. His father, Ezekiel Haslett, was the founder of the company, and the company, as I told you, is virtually all there is to Cloverville.

"Haslett was unmarried at the time of his death, but he left two half brothers, Bruce Jasper and Norman Jasper.

"Rumor has it that there's a will leaving everything to the Jaspers unless Haslett left issue.

"That is a peculiar provision in the will, because although Haslett was once married, so far as is known he never had any children.

"Now, then, I give you rank gossip, but this is a story that my operative ferreted out.

"Many years ago, during his flaming youth, Harmon Haslett got a girl in 'trouble,' as they said in the parlance of the times.

"The girl was all right as far as that end of it was concerned, but she wasn't society and Haslett was the *crème de la crème* of Cloverville. He was supposed to make a marriage with some wealthy social queen and all that sort of stuff.

"Haslett got in a panic when he found out about the girl, and he went to Garland—our old friend Slick Garland, the troubleshooter for the company, the man who is supposed to keep the public image intact.

"At that time Harmon's father, Ezekiel Haslett, would have raised the roof if he had known that his son had a girl in trouble.

"Good old Garland was the worldly-wise man of the picture. Apparently he said to the kid, 'Now, take it easy, buddy; this is something that can happen to anyone.

" 'I'll tell you what you do. You get on the next boat for Europe. Stay over there for a year if necessary. At the same time I'll send your girl friend a thousand dollars. That's the smart way to take care of it.' "

"How did you hear this?" Mason asked Drake.

"Through my operative, who, in turn, had it from a person to whom Haslett had confided the secret of his past.

"Everything worked out the way it was supposed to.

Haslett went to Europe; the troubleshooter sent the girl —whose name, incidentally, was never mentioned to the person in whom Haslett confided—a thousand dollars in crisp new hundred-dollar bills in a plain, unmarked envelope.

"The girl took the money and disappeared. Up to that point everything went according to schedule.

"There was only one flaw: the girl didn't come back.

"Now that started worrying Haslett. He felt that if the girl had had things fixed up, within the course of time she would have returned. But she never came back. Her parents apparently had never heard from her, and eventually they moved away. I believe the father died and the mother remarried.

"Haslett felt that somewhere he might have an illegitimate child. He spent money trying to find some trace of the girl. He couldn't get even a clue.

"Now, then, the half brothers want to be able to prove that there never was any child—or if there was a child, they want to prove that it wasn't Haslett's child.

"Their idea is to locate the woman in the case, to get her to confide in some clever female operative, and to find out what happened to the illegitimate child; and if the child is still alive, they want to be able to prove that the father was someone other than Haslett.

"Haslett never even intimated that the child wasn't his, although the troubleshooter, good old Slick Garland, kept implanting doubts in Haslett's mind."

"He could trust Garland to protect his secret?" Mason asked.

"Apparently Garland was one of those troubleshooters

who knew what to do and went ahead and did it and then knew how to keep his mouth shut."

"Looking at it from young Haslett's point of view, you can see the logic of the situation and the fact that he was getting sound advice," Mason said.

"Does anyone look at it from the girl's point of view?" Della asked.

"Apparently Garland did," Drake said; "but he just may have sized her up a hundred per cent wrong."

Mason glanced at Della Street.

"The fact that she never returned home, never kept in touch with her parents, is certainly indicative of the fact that she didn't do what they planned for her to do."

Mason and Della Street exchanged glances.

"Now, then," Drake went on, "you're dealing with some mysterious woman. You substituted a ringer, a decoy. You haven't told me anything about the case, other than that you wanted a decoy of a certain description. I furnished you that decoy. I don't know anything about the case except what you've told me and what I've reported to you. I imagine you can't tell me anything more without betraying the confidence of a client, but here's the information. I've dumped it in your lap."

Paul Drake got to his feet. "All right, Perry," he said, "this is official notification that even with trade discounts your client's two hundred dollars is long gone and your additional two hundred just disappeared around the corner. Now, then, do I discontinue everything?"

"That would mean having your operative move out of the apartment?"

"Sure," Drake said. "I'm paying her a per diem and all

of her expenses. I'm doing this job for you at cost and maybe a little less."

"Don't," Mason said. "Bill me at regular prices, Paul."

"And what do I do about discontinuing?"

"Keep on until I tell you to stop," Mason said. "I'm enjoying this tremendously; and somehow I have a hunch, Paul, that all of the information we can collect at this time is going to prove very valuable later on."

"Will contest?" Drake asked. "That's somewhat out of your line, isn't it?"

Mason said, "I'm a trial lawyer, Paul. I go into court on anything where there's a contest. I've specialized in criminal cases. I've done some personal-injury work. I have tried a will contest now and then. Wherever there's a fight, I'm apt to be in the middle of it."

"Well," Drake said, "you could have a fight in this case. I'll keep on, Perry, but it's going to cost money."

"I've got money."

Drake laughed. "You also have the damnedest sense of adventure."

"And," Mason said, "I have a sense of justice. When I see all of these people pitted against . . . Oh, well, never mind."

Drake grinned. "I'm not doing any speculating, Perry. I don't even want to know where you have the real girl stashed away, but I can warn you to be careful. Garland is one hell of a smart operator. Jarmen Dayton is no slouch. You may have those people fooled for a while, but be careful they don't turn the tables on you."

"I'll be careful," Mason promised.

Chapter Six

It was shortly before closing time in the afternoon when the phone from the outer office rang and Della Street, answering it, raised her eyebrows in surprise, glanced at Perry Mason, said into the phone, "Just a minute, Gertie; I'll let you know."

She turned to the lawyer. "Stephen L. Garland is in the outer office, says he has no appointment, that he wants to see you upon a matter of business in which he has reason to believe you're already interested."

"Good old Slick Garland," Mason said. "The trouble-shooter, the smart one! Now, what do you suppose *he* wants?"

"Information," Della Street said.

"But this is such a peculiar way to get it," Mason said. "Garland should be the sort who taps telephone lines, who bribes witnesses, who— Anyway, Della, go get him. Let's see what he has to say for himself."

A few moments later Della ushered the tall, cadaverous, unsmiling Garland into the office.

"Mr. Mason," Garland said in a deep, bass voice.

"Sit down," the lawyer invited.

"You know who I am and all about me," Garland said.

Mason raised his eyebrows.

"Let's not play innocent with each other, Mason. Time is very definitely *not* on our side. I think the time has come to be absolutely frank with each other."

"Go ahead; it's your move," Mason said.

Garland said, "For many, many years I've been a troubleshooter for the Cloverville Spring and Suspension Company.

"Originally I was a claims adjuster; then I graduated into assisting attorneys in damage suits; then I became a troubleshooter, more or less in charge of public relations."

Mason nodded.

"Now, then," Garland went on, "you have a woman, in whom I am vitally interested, as a client. You have her salted away. You think I don't know where she is. I do."

"Indeed," Mason said.

"She's in the Rosa Lee Apartments, apartment three-ten. She's going under the name of Ellen Smith. Actually her name is Ellen Calvert. I did her a bad turn some twenty years ago. I'm sorry about it. I've lived to regret it, but a man can't bat a hundred per cent when he gets into a big-league ball team."

"You are playing big-league ball?" Mason asked.

"The biggest."

"Such as what?"

"I had a job," Garland said. "I tried my best to do

that job and do it well. The head of the company was
Ezekiel Haslett. He was a tough, square-jawed, thin-
mouthed product of the old school.

"Heaven knows what the kids in his generation really
were like. I guess they were repressed, disciplined, and
worked so hard that they didn't have time for any animal
spirits.

"Ezekiel wanted the public image of the Cloverville
Spring and Suspension Company to be the highest. It was
up to me to keep it that way.

"One of the employees would be in trouble over drunk
driving. I had to square it so there was no publicity. One
time one of the guys got drunk and raped one of the employees. I had to square that—and, believe me, it was a
job. She was all set to prosecute. But I pointed out to her
that under the peculiar provisions of the law the minute
she claimed that she had been forcibly attacked the defense had a right to show her previous sexual experience,
if any—all of it.

"She tried to bluff it out. She said that it didn't make a
bit of difference to her. But that was where old Garland
had been on the job earning his salary. I'd done a lot of
gumshoe work. I was able to point out names, dates and
telephone numbers. Then I gave her a thousand dollars
in cash to satisfy her injured feelings, arranged to get her
a job with one of the companies that we dealt with in a
distant city, and shipped her off with a prepaid ticket and
my blessing.

"In the end I think she felt good about it."

"And this other young woman that you're talking
about?" Mason asked.

"There I botched things," Garland said, "although I followed the same procedure that was standard in cases of that sort. She had been in love with young Haslett. Things had gone pretty far, and she found herself pregnant.

"Mind you, that was a while ago. She talked about 'shame' and she absolutely refused to do the things that are more or less taken for granted these days."

"What did she want?" Mason asked.

"I've no idea what she wanted. At the time, I assumed that she wanted Haslett to marry her and to have the child. But now I think she was just so completely panic-stricken that she didn't know what she did want. Anyway, I did the usual. I sent young Haslett off to Europe on a prolonged tour where no one knew where he was and it would take a person with money to find him. Then I sent her a thousand dollars in hundred-dollar bills in a plain, unmarked envelope.

"Of course, if she had wanted to make a squawk, I'd have denied all knowledge of sending her the money and she couldn't have proven a thing.

"That's almost always a winning combination. They may start out being indignant, but before they are through they get practical. They sit down and count those ten hundred-dollar bills. They can get fixed up for a couple of hundred if they know where to go. They seldom have to pay more than four hundred. That leaves them with at least six hundred dollars. It gives them carfare to any place within reason they want to go. It gives them money while they're getting a new job, and they stay for a few months, then come back home with a story about a loss of memory or an irresistible desire to see the world, a set of fictitious adventures, and they pick up the threads of life where they left off.

"Sometimes they meet a new man and return to introduce their friends and parents to a stalwart, beaming husband who probably knows absolutely nothing about the past."

"It didn't work in this case?" Mason asked.

"It didn't work. I don't know just what happened, but I know where the girl is and I want to talk with her. You've got her stashed away. It's only a question of time until I get her and get to talk with her."

"You're certain of that?" Mason asked.

"I'll tell you how certain I am," Garland said. "Haslett has been lost at sea. If there's an heir, the heir inherits. If there isn't an heir, the half brothers inherit. The half brothers are out on the trail, trying to find out what happened. I'm an employee of the company. I'm going to be working for the half brothers or I'm going to be working for an heir. It doesn't make too much difference which: I'll try to do my job.

"However, I do want to know where I stand, and I want to bring this case to a satisfactory conclusion by being the one that cracks it and not having some private detective employed by the half brothers beat my time."

"What," Mason asked, "specifically, do they want me to do?"

Garland said, "There are lots of people involved, and they have different wants. The half brothers, represented by Duncan Lovett, want to prove there never was any illegitimate child. Then the half brothers inherit the plant and I find myself with three years to go, working for the half brothers, before I can retire on a pension.

"Put yourself in my position, Mason. I'm not going to do anything which will antagonize the half brothers.

"On the other hand, let us suppose that there was an illegitimate child and that rumor is correct and Harmon Haslett has made a will leaving everything to that illegitimate child if the parentage can be established.

"That child would be about nineteen years old now. That child would inherit the company. I'd find myself in an entirely different position."

"And so you come to me?" Mason asked.

"So I come to you," Garland said.

"You know that I'm bound by professional ethics, that I can't give you any information?"

"I know you're bound by professional ethics. I know you can't give me any information. But I also know that you weren't born yesterday. You're probably the only one who knows the facts and . . ."

There was a sharp, insistent ringing on Mason's unlisted telephone, the phone to which only Della Street and Paul Drake possessed the number.

Della Street raised her eyebrows at Mason.

The lawyer nodded, said, "I'll take it myself, Della," picked up the telephone and said, "What is it, Paul?"

"This decoy of yours is in trouble," Drake said.

"How come?"

"A lawyer by the name of Lovett and some woman who is with him have got into the apartment."

"Dammit," Mason said. "I left instructions that she wasn't to let anyone in."

"They engineered this too cleverly," Drake said. "The woman knocked at the door. My operative opened it just to the limit of the safety chain. The woman was standing outside; a man was in the background carrying a big box which appeared to be filled with tools. The woman said, 'My apartment is right below yours, and there's a bad leak which we think is coming from a faulty connection in your bathtub. In any event, my ceiling is soaked with water. We've got to shut off your water for a few minutes.'

"My operative should have had her head examined, but she fell for it, took the chain off the door, and said, 'Come in.' The man brought the box in and put it down. It was filled with old newspapers and a briefcase. He took out the briefcase and said, 'Now, my dear, I want to ask you a few questions. If you answer them truthfully, everything will be all right. If you lie, you are going to be in serious trouble.' "

"So what happened?"

"My operative refused to talk, ordered the people out of the apartment. They are still sitting there. She wants to know whether to call the police or what to do."

"Call her back," Mason said. "Tell her to wait right there until I get there. We'll be there within twenty minutes. She can tell these people that Perry Mason is coming to represent her. That probably will frighten them out. In case it doesn't, we'll see what they have to say when we get there."

Mason slammed down the receiver, said to Della Street, "Grab a notebook, Della; let's go."

The lawyer paused, looking at Garland.

"All right, Garland," he said; "you've been casing an

apartment in the Rosa Lee Apartments. A woman known to you as Ellen Smith is in there, and some people have forced their way into the apartment."

"That probably will be Duncan Z. Lovett," Garland said. "He's clever and he's fast. He has a private detective on the job who knows as much as I do. We were casing the apartment together. You're bucking money in this thing, Mason, and you're bucking brains."

"All right," Mason said, "if you want a free ride, come along. I may want a witness to what's going to happen."

"Remember I'm biased," Garland said.

"You're biased," Mason told him, "but you're not going to commit perjury and you're not going to testify to something that didn't happen. I have an idea you're a square shooter."

Garland said, "All right, since we're putting cards on the table, Mason, I'll tell you this. I try to shoot square, but I have loyalty to the people I represent and I'm tricky."

Mason grinned, said, "Come on, let's go. I'm tricky myself."

"Jarmen Dayton is already out there casing the apartment," Garland said.

"Fine; we'll pick him up and let him come in. We need an audience. The more the merrier. You can go with us in my car. I'm going to push pretty hard on the throttle."

Garland got to his feet. "Let's go."

Chapter Seven

MASON parked his car at the curb in front of the Rosa Lee Apartments and slid from behind the steering wheel.

His two passengers jerked open the doors and got out. Della carried a briefcase filled with notebooks and ball-point pens.

Stephen Garland looked swiftly around. "There's Dayton," he said. "Do you want him?"

"We want him," Mason said.

Garland gave a signal.

The heavyset private detective opened the door on the side of the curb and stepped to the sidewalk.

Mason walked up to him. "We're going up, Dayton. You want to go with us?"

Dayton hesitated a moment, then said, "Why not?" He looked inquisitively at Garland.

"Mason is hep," Garland said. "I think we're starting a brand-new deal. Let's each one of us go his own way from here on in."

"Suits me," Dayton said.

The four of them entered the apartment house, climbed the stairs to the Drake apartment where Drake's operative was living under the name of Ellen Smith.

Mason knocked on the door.

The door was opened a cautious two inches, then held in place by a chain.

Drake's operative looked out at them, then, her face showing relief, threw the chain back and opened the door.

"Come in," she invited.

Mason said, "I am Perry Mason. These men are Stephen Lockley Garland and Jarmen Dayton. The young woman is my secretary, Miss Della Street."

A wiry, pinched-faced man in the fifties, with a sharp-pointed nose and beady black eyes which were quite close together, came rushing forward with extended hand.

"Mr. Mason," he said, "this is really a pleasure and an honor. I am Duncan Z. Lovett of the firm of Lovett, Price and Maxwell. I am representing Bruce Jasper and Norman Jasper, who are half brothers of Harmon Haslett, who has recently been lost at sea in a tragic shipwreck.

"I am investigating a fraud. I know of your reputation. I know of your outstanding ability, and I also know that you are too ethical to want to be mixed up in a fraud. I am glad indeed that this woman telephoned for you to come.

"I know the two gentlemen with you. I am glad to meet you, Miss Street. And may I introduce this lady with me? She is Maxine Edfield. She resides in Cloverville. She is —and has been for some time—a client of mine. I have represented her in several matters.

"You will note that I am giving you *all* of the facts.

"Now, then, if we can all sit down, I would like to have Miss Edfield tell you a story. I think when she finishes her recital we will have the atmosphere cleared and will perhaps be in a position to talk business and perhaps to become good friends."

Maxine Edfield, a woman of about forty—with sharp gray eyes; an alert, aggressive manner; a spare frame; and a long, thin mouth which even copious lipstick couldn't quite turn into a rosebud—said in a harsh, metallic voice, "Hello, everybody."

"Tell them your story, Maxine," Lovett said.

"All of it?" she asked.

"All of it."

Maxine Edfield said somewhat defiantly, "I'm a working girl."

Mason smiled encouragingly.

"So am I," Della Street said with a friendly smile.

Maxine said, "I never had enough money to put me through a secretarial school or to get any kind of a decent education. I've waited tables. I've worked up to being a cashier at the Cloverville Café. It's a pretty good job."

"And how do you happen to be here?" Mason asked.

"I came on a plane with Mr. Lovett. Mr. Lovett is attorney for the people who operate the Cloverville Café, and he arranged for me to get away."

"Never mind any more preliminaries," Lovett said; "just go ahead and tell them your story, Maxine. When did you first meet this woman who now tells us that her name is Ellen Smith?"

THE CASE OF THE QUEENLY CONTESTANT

"I met her way back—let's see, it was twenty years ago, before the kid was even thinking of beauty contests."

"How well did you know her?"

"I knew her quite well."

"You are now talking about this woman sitting next to me, the one on whose shoulder I am placing my hand?" Mason asked.

"That's right."

"What's her name?" Lovett asked.

"Ellen Calvert."

"How well did you know her?"

"I knew her very well. We exchanged confidences from time to time. She used to eat in the café where I was slinging hash, and after I got to know her I saw that she got a little more on the plate than was customary. I kept her coffee cup filled with hot coffee, and sometimes when business was slack I'd sit down at the table and talk with her for a while."

"Did you know her other than in the restaurant?" Lovett asked.

"I'll say I did. After a while we got friendly and she invited me up to her room and I invited her to mine. She was a beautiful kid, only a little bit too tall, and I'm the one that told her how to handle herself. I said, 'Dearie, hold your chin up. Try to be even taller than you are.' Most tall girls try to wear flat heels and squeeze themselves down into their clothes so they can look an inch or so shorter, and all they do is manage to look stooped.

"A tall girl who is proud of being tall and stands perfectly straight gets a queenly carriage that helps a lot. Lots of people like tall girls.

"She told me she didn't like to be tall because it embarrassed her to dance with a man who was shorter than she was, and I told her to get over it, and I kept counseling her on how to stand."

"Go ahead," Lovett said. "Tell us the rest of it. Get to the emotional part."

"Well," Maxine said, "we went out a couple of times on dates together. Ellen was a good scout. She was fun to be with on a foursome and she was—well, she wasn't too prudish."

"Never mind, never mind that," Lovett interrupted hurriedly. "You can skip that. Tell us the part about her confiding in you about her love affair."

"Which one?"

"You know the one."

"You mean the Haslett affair?"

"Go ahead," Lovett said.

"Well, she got a job in the Cloverville Spring and Suspension Company and young Haslett noticed her. That is, he was young at that time. He was about twenty-two, I guess, and I think Ellen was eighteen.

"Of course, Harmon Haslett was the catch of the town. He'd just returned from college, where he'd graduated, and he was settling down to follow in his father's footsteps in the Spring and Suspension Company.

"Well, Ellen went out with Harmon Haslett a couple of times. They had to be awfully cautious about it, because old Ezekiel Haslett, Harmon's father, would have raised merry hell if he'd had any inkling that Harmon was going out with one of the girls in the office.

"Old Ezekiel was one of those self-righteous individuals

who seldom crack a smile. I doubt if he'd ever done any necking in his life before he got married, and he—well, he was a pill."

"Go on," Lovett said.

"Well, things got pretty torrid between Ellen here and Harmon Haslett, and then I guess Harmon realized what he was getting into and he began to pull back.

"That was when Ellen came to me for advice. She said that maybe she'd been a little too easy and gone a little too far a little too soon and that she was now certain Harmon Haslett was very definitely not contemplating matrimony but—well, he was still interested and crazy about her when he was with her, but when he wasn't with her he was very definitely—well, you can get the picture. I don't have to spell it out for you."

"Go ahead," Lovett said.

"So Ellen confided in me that she thought she'd try and force a marriage by telling him she was pregnant. I told her that that would probably shipwreck the whole affair. But she said it was not going the way she wanted it and—"

"All this is a dirty lie!" Drake's operative exclaimed.

"Keep quiet," Mason said. "Don't say a word, Ellen. Let's just hear this thing out."

"Go on," Lovett said. "You can express things as delicately as possible; but, after all, this is a legal matter and we can't have any ambiguities."

"Well," Maxine said, "the long and short of it is she told him she was pregnant."

"Was she?"

"Hell, no!"

"Do you know?"

"I know."

"And what happened?"

"She wanted him to marry her. She pulled the sweet-young-thing line on him and pointed out that her life had been ruined and it was up to him to take care of her and do the right thing."

"And then?"

"Harmon Haslett went into a tailspin. He was afraid of the responsibility. He was afraid his father would find out. He was in a spot. So he turned to the troubleshooter. I think that's you, Mr. Garland."

Garland sat perfectly impassive, saying nothing.

"So young Haslett suggested that it might be possible for the troubleshooter to arrange for Ellen to see a doctor who would fix her up; and the troubleshooter told Harmon that that would be the last thing he'd want to see happen, that the minute Harmon mixed into anything like that he was laying himself wide open for trouble, that if things didn't go just right he'd be in hot water and if things did turn out all right he'd be in a spot where he could be blackmailed.

"So this troubleshooter told Harmon Haslett to let him handle the whole thing.

"The troubleshooter went to Ezekiel and told the old man that he thought it would be a good plan if Harmon went to Europe for an indefinite stay to look over some of the European markets and broaden out his perspective a little bit.

"I don't know just how much he told Ezekiel, but Ezekiel got the idea, and the next thing anybody knew Harmon Haslett was off for Europe.

"At that time Ellen here got an envelope in the mail which contained ten one-hundred-dollar bills. There was nothing else in it—just ten one-hundred-dollar bills."

"Did she tell you about it? Did you see the money?"

"She told me about it and I saw the money," Maxine said. "And she told me that she'd made a play and lost out on the jackpot but that she had still won the consolation prize, that she had a thousand bucks and she was going to ditch the whole business, go to a new place where she wasn't known and start all over again."

"She told you that?"

"She told me that."

"This woman?" Lovett asked.

"This woman," Maxine said.

Lovett looked around and said, "For your information, Maxine Edfield has made an affidavit containing these statements. I have that affidavit in my possession. I don't think anyone wants to get mixed up in a fraudulent claim, except perhaps Ellen Calvert here may have tried—or may have had some vague idea . . . But I'm satisfied you'll drop it now, won't you, my dear?"

Drake's operative looked to Mason for instructions.

Mason said, "Say nothing."

"Can't I even deny . . ."

"Not yet," Mason said. "You are keeping silent at the request of counsel."

Duncan Lovett smiled. "I can readily understand that counsel would be embarrassed by any statement from you at this time. In view of the statement by Maxine Edfield, I feel that the case is closed."

"I'd like to ask Miss Edfield some questions," Mason said.

"Go right ahead," Lovett said.

Jarmen Dayton warned, "You let this lawyer start cross-examining this witness and pretty quick you won't have any witness."

"Nonsense," Lovett said; "the witness has told her story. She's going to tell it on the witness stand if she has to. When she tells it on the witness stand, she'll be cross-examined. If she can't stand a little cross-examination now, she can't stand it then. I have repeatedly told her to tell the truth and nothing but the truth, and then there is nothing to be afraid of. Isn't that right, Maxine?"

"That's right, Mr. Lovett."

Lovett smiled at Mason. "Go ahead and ask your questions," he said.

Stephen Garland took a package of cigarettes from his pocket. "Anyone mind if I smoke?"

No one made any objection.

Garland lit the cigarette, said, "How many questions do you want to ask, Mr. Mason?"

"Just a few," Mason said.

"I'm neutral," Garland said. "Sitting in a corner, so to speak."

Jarmen Dayton said, "Don't kid yourself, Garland. We're the innocent bystanders who are going to get hit by the stray bullets."

Garland grinned, said, "That's a chance we have to take. There's no place to duck now."

"What questions did you want to ask, Mr. Mason?" Maxine Edfield said. "I'm perfectly willing to answer any and all questions at any time. I've been a working girl all of my life. I'm a human being. I've had a few purple passages myself, but I've always made an honest living and I never made any money except from working."

"Very commendable," Mason said. "I wasn't going to inquire into your background, Miss Edfield. I just wanted to ask you a couple of questions about things that seemed to require explanation."

"Such as what?"

"Well, you said that Ellen Calvert had taken the thousand dollars and gone to a new place where she wasn't known."

"That's right."

"How do you know that?"

"From what she told me."

"What I am getting at," Mason said, "is why she would do a thing like that."

"Why not? She was young. She had life before her. She had a thousand bucks in her stocking. The world was her oyster. Believe me, if someone had given me a thousand dollars when I was that old I'd have shaken the dust of Cloverville from my feet and taken the first train out of town."

"I'm afraid you don't get what I'm driving at," Mason said. "Here was Ellen Calvert, winner of a beauty contest, holder of some papers entitling her to a screen test, and—"

"Oh, I get you now," Maxine interrupted. "Sure, she had the world by the tail on a downhill pull. Your idea is there was no reason for her to duck out."

"That's right."

"Well," Maxine said, "you're looking at it one way. Now try looking at it the other way. Here was Ellen, who had been within an ace of landing the most eligible bachelor in Cloverville. She probably counted on it pretty strong.

"When the affair began to cool off, she decided to stake everything on the turn of a card. She pulled this pregnancy gag and wanted to see if it would work.

"It didn't work.

"She woke up with the realization that she had irrevocably lost the man she wanted. Personally, I think she was really in love with him. I mean really and truly. But a girl has to look out for herself, and Ellen had been around enough to know that.

"Anyway, she had been to Hollywood. She'd taken her screen tests. She thought she was going to hear from them for a while, but she was beginning to wake up to the fact that this was one of these situations where they say, 'Don't call me; we'll call you.'

"In other words, provision had been made for a couple of screen tests. The people who were obligated to furnish those screen tests had carried out their share of the contract, which consisted of doing nothing more than putting Ellen up in front of a camera, letting her recite lines from a script, portray certain emotions to the best of her ability, and then step down.

"It was fun while it lasted and, of course, she had high hopes. She thought she did a swell job of registering rage, hatred, love, astonishment, terror, and all that stuff. Actually, from the standpoint of Hollywood studios, which are accustomed to judging professional actresses, all Ellen was doing was standing up in front of a camera and making faces.

"As soon as they saw the tests they knew the answer, but they didn't dash Ellen's hopes all at once. They told her, 'Go on back to Cloverville and we'll evaluate the tests. Don't call us; we'll call you.'

"That was when Ellen began to see her little house of cards falling apart; and right at that time she thought that her boyfriend was beginning to cool off, that he was still ardent and impetuous but he was beginning more and more to think about what was going to happen when his father, old Ezekiel Haslett, found out that his son had been playing around with one of the girls in the organization, that the affair had gone a lot further than the father would approve of, and that Ellen had her hopes set on marriage.

"When Harmon Haslett was with Ellen he was all enthused, but as soon as he'd leave Ellen he lost his enthusiasm mighty fast."

"You think Ellen knew this?" Mason asked.

Maxine laughed. "She's sitting right there beside you. Why don't you ask *her?* Of course she knew it. That's the trouble with you smart lawyers; you know all about law but you don't know enough about human nature. You underestimate women.

"When a man is with a woman he portrays his inner thoughts by a thousand and one little things—emotions, glances of the eye, the tone of voice in which he says things, the spacing of his words. . . . Of course Ellen knew it."

"How do you know she knew it?"

"Because she told me all about it. All about how Harmon was having spells of moody silence, how he wasn't calling her quite as frequently as he used to, how—when he would be with her—he would try to keep things under control so he could gradually break away. But, of course, he couldn't, and then he'd be affectionate and pleading and loving and all that. But the handwriting was there on the wall.

"So when Ellen found she'd lost him—and by that time realized that she was going to be humiliated by not having any of the Hollywood contracts materialize—Ellen was a pretty disillusioned young woman.

"Then she suddenly had a thousand dollars in hundred-dollar bills handed to her with no strings attached, and Ellen just up and took off. It's what I'd have done under similar circumstances. It's what anyone would have done."

"You knew Ellen quite well?"

"Of course I knew her well. One girl doesn't confide about her love affairs and her idea of working the pregnancy racket to a complete stranger."

"I didn't suggest you were a complete stranger," Mason said. "I wanted to know how well you knew her."

"Well, I knew her just as well as one girl can know another."

"And this is the woman sitting next to me?"

"That's the woman sitting next to you, and don't try to deny it," Maxine said. "She's changed a lot, but she's the same Ellen Calvert."

"And this is the girl that told you all of these things about trying to trap Harmon Haslett by pretending to be pregnant?"

"That's the one," Maxine said, "and don't let her try to lie out of it or pull the wool over your eyes."

"Now just a minute, just a minute," Duncan Lovett said. "The identity of this woman doesn't enter into the situation at the present time. She hasn't denied her identity."

Mason said, "In a situation of this kind questions looking to the accuracy of the recollection of the witness are never out of order."

"I understand, I understand," Lovett said. Then he added with a grin. "It is just that I had expected a more skillful type of cross-examination. Not that I'm making any criticism, Counselor. It is simply the fact that your reputation for brilliance in cross-examination is such that I expected—well, I don't know—a lot of razzle-dazzle, I guess."

"Razzle-dazzle is not good cross-examination," Mason said. "The purpose of cross-examination is to find out whether a witness is telling the truth."

Lovett laughed sarcastically. "That's the line they try to teach you in the lawbooks and in the colleges. Actually, when you come right down to it, you know and I know, Mason, that the object of cross-examination is first to find out to your own satisfaction if a witness is telling the truth. If you find out the witness *is* telling the truth, then you go on to the next step—which is to try and confuse the witness so that any testimony the witness has given is open to doubt."

"And you thought I would do something like that?" Mason asked.

"As far as I'm concerned," Lovett said, "your reputation has been such that I thought you would perform a Hindu rope trick."

Mason said, "I'm sorry to disappoint you."

"Well, go right ahead with your cross-examination or whatever it is you call it," Lovett said.

"I am at the moment concentrating on the recollection of the witness," Mason said. "It seems to me that there might be some case for a confusion of identity after a lapse of some twenty years."

"Oh, bosh and nonsense," Lovett said. "She recognized Ellen Calvert the minute she saw her, the minute the woman came to the door. She said, 'Hello, Ellen.' Isn't that true, Ellen?"

"Don't answer any questions at the moment," Mason cautioned Drake's operative.

"Well," Lovett said, "as far as I'm concerned, you're wasting a lot of time on a question of identity."

"Well, let me ask you this question, Miss Edfield," Mason said. "I'll put it in the conventional way. Are you as certain of the identity of Ellen Calvert as you are of any of the other statements you have made?"

"Absolutely."

"If you are mistaken in the identity of Ellen Calvert, then you could be mistaken in your recollection as to any or all of the other testimony?"

"Now wait a minute, wait a minute," Lovett said suddenly, getting to his feet. "What is this? What's cooking?"

"Do you object to Miss Edfield's answering that question?" Mason asked.

"Well, I don't like the way you're putting the question. I don't like . . . Maxine, this is Ellen Calvert all right?"

"Of course it is."

"You're sure?"

"Of course I'm sure. This man isn't going to bamboozle me by pretending this isn't Ellen Calvert. I guess I know her and I guess I know what he's trying to do. Just all that business of asking me if I could be mistaken about the other things I've testified to, if I'm mistaken about this being Ellen Calvert. It's all part of that hocus-pocus you warned me about before we left Cloverville."

Lovett glanced at Mason's operative, then back at Maxine Edfield, then slowly took his seat.

"Let's have it clearly understood," Mason said, "that if you're mistaken in the identity of this person as being Ellen Calvert, you could be mistaken in the other parts of your statement."

"Baloney!" she said. "That's Ellen Calvert, and I've told you the story just the way it happened."

Mason turned to Drake's operative. "Will the real Ellen Calvert please stand up?" he said.

There was sudden tense silence.

Mason said to Drake's operative, "Now, will you please tell us your real name and occupation?"

"You mean it?" the operative asked.

"I mean it," Mason said.

"My real name is Jessie Alva," she said. "I am a licensed private detective and I am employed by the Drake Detective Agency. I was employed a short time ago to come to Mr. Mason's office, stay for a few minutes, then leave and come to this apartment.

"This apartment is leased by the Drake Detective Agency. Is there anything else, Mr. Mason?"

"I think that covers it," Mason said.

Lovett jumped to his feet. "You have deliberately tricked us."

"Wasn't that what you expected?" Mason asked. "You seemed disappointed at the conventional nature of my cross-examination. I am sorry I didn't live up to expectations."

Maxine Edfield said, "He's lying. They're all lying. Don't let them kid you. That's Ellen Calvert!"

"You have your ID card with you, Miss Alva?" Mason asked.

The operative nodded, produced a billfold with credit cards, driver's license, and an ID card as a private detective.

Duncan Lovett went through those cards carefully, studying each one, looking at the photographs on the cards, comparing them with the face of the operative.

Slowly, reluctantly, he closed the folder and returned it to the woman.

Jarmen Dayton said, "I told you so. You turn that guy loose and he's going to have things all tied up in knots."

Lovett said, "This still doesn't affect the validity of our claim. This isn't producing any heir."

Maxine Edfield said, "It's a trap. He's given this witness a phony identification. How do you know Ellen Calvert didn't come out here and take the name of Jessie Alva and go to work as a private detective? Just the fact that she's now got a driver's license under the name of Jessie Alva doesn't mean she isn't really Ellen Calvert."

Duncan Lovett became apprehensive. "A great deal depends, Maxine, on your recognition, your . . ."

"Of course I recognize her. She hasn't changed that much. She's still got the same stuck-up method of holding her chin up and trying to act like a queen. She's older now than when I used to double-date with her, but she hasn't changed a damn bit. You let this Perry Mason start twisting you around his finger and he'll have you jumping through hoops."

Lovett became thoughtfully silent.

Jarmen Dayton said, "How about you, Garland?"

Garland grinned. "As far as I am concerned, I am sitting on the sidelines. But I'm the one that is responsible for this debacle. I made the fatal mistake of underestimating my adversary.

"Of course, the only identification I had was an old photograph taken twenty years ago and a description that she was unusually tall and had a rather dignified, regal air about her. When I baited Perry Mason into sending for his client and this woman came to his office and left and I tailed her here—well, I admit that, now I think back on it, it was just too darned easy. You don't tangle with Perry Mason and come off that easy."

Dayton said, "You don't think she's Ellen Calvert?"

Garland laughed and said, "If she's Ellen Calvert, I'm Napoleon Bonaparte."

Maxine Edfield screamed, "You can't gyp me out of my money that easy! Of course she's Ellen Calvert!"

Mason glanced significantly at Della Street, who had been taking notes.

"What do you mean 'gyp you out of your money,' Maxine?"

"That guy Lovett was going to pay me—"

"Shut up!" Lovett shouted. "You damn fool, keep your trap shut!"

Maxine Edfield suddenly became silent.

"You got that down, Della?" Mason asked.

"Every word of it," Della said.

Mason grinned. "I think we can all go home now."

"Now just a minute, just a minute," Lovett said. "I don't want those last statements misinterpreted. I agreed to pay Maxine Edfield her expenses out here and a hundred dollars a day for the time she was here. I did not agree to pay her for any testimony."

Mason smiled politely. "I think," he said, "my prior remarks still stand and we can adjourn the meeting.

"As far as you're concerned, Miss Alva, you can report to Paul Drake that you've done everything you were hired to do, that you're vacating the apartment. And thank you very much for your cooperation."

Mason arose, walked to the corridor door, held it open, smiled and said, "This way out."

Chapter Eight

Mason and Della Street left the elevator and walked down the long corridor toward Mason's offices.

"Do we stop in and say hello to Paul Drake?" Della Street asked.

Mason shook his head. "No. Drake will have received a report from his operative, Jessie Alva. He'll know that the case is terminated as far as he's concerned."

"And as far as we're concerned?"

Mason grinned. "Well, we had a dramatic conclusion anyway."

Della Street laughed. "I'll never forget the expression on that lawyer's face when he had so patronizingly stated that he had expected more from you in the line of cross-examination and then suddenly realized that you had trapped his witness and his whole case had blown up in his face."

Mason said thoughtfully, "Of course, Della, the fact that Maxine Edfield made a mistake in the identity of

Ellen Calvert *actually* doesn't discredit her whole testimony."

"But the way you trapped her into the admission it does," Della Street said.

"That," Mason told her, fitting his key to the lock on the door to his private office, "is only one thing. Her admission of receiving payment for her testimony is going to hurt that side of the case more than anything."

The lawyer opened the door, held it for Della, then entered behind her, removed his key, and closed the door.

"Of course, Maxine Edfield *could* have been telling the truth. She was too eager to be of service to Duncan Lovett. And when Lovett assured her that they had run Ellen Calvert to earth and they went to the apartment and the door was opened by a tall woman with a queenly bearing who matched the general description of Ellen Calvert, Maxine naturally jumped to an erroneous conclusion.

"After all, she had the word of Duncan Lovett, of Stephen Garland, and of Jarmen Dayton that this was the person they were looking for."

Della Street said, "Gertie's still working. I'd better report to her that we're here."

She picked up the telephone to the outer office, said, "We're back, Gertie. If there's anyone . . . what? . . . WHAT!

"Good heavens!" Della said. "Hang on!"

She turned to Perry Mason and said, "The real Ellen Calvert is in the office impatiently waiting to see you."

"Good lord!" Mason said. "Now we *will* have a field day!"

"Do you suppose Garland and Dayton are still watching the office?" Della Street asked.

"They'd hardly expect me to be so foolish as to send for my client now," Mason said thoughtfully. "And they'd hardly expect Ellen to be so foolish as to come in, but—well, we're in for it now, Della. Tell Gertie to have her come in."

Della Street passed the message over the telephone to the receptionist, and a few seconds later Ellen Adair opened the door to the private office.

"I'm sorry, Mr. Mason," she said, "but I simply had to see you. I've changed my mind."

"You've chosen a mighty poor time to change your mind," Mason said. "Sit down."

"Why?" she asked. "What's so bad about the time?"

Mason said, "As I suppose you are aware, Harmon Haslett has been lost at sea in the wreck of a private yacht. Stephen Garland, the troubleshooter for the company, and Jarmen Dayton, a detective, came out here to try and locate you. They knew that you had been in my office. They assumed you would come again.

"I anticipated their moves and hired a female detective of about your age and build, gave her instructions in the mannerisms she was to assume, and staked her out in an apartment.

"We have just come from that apartment, where we had a dramatic scene. An attorney named Duncan Z. Lovett brought a witness—a Maxine Edfield—who identified the female detective as you and stated that you and she had double-dated and that you had confided in her after your love affair with Harmon Haslett, that you were worried because you thought Harmon was cooling off and you decided, after conferring with Maxine Edfield, to pretend that you were pregnant and see if you couldn't force Haslett into marriage.

"In place of that scheme's working, she said, Haslett left abruptly for Europe, acting on the advice of Garland, the troubleshooter. She said that Garland sent you a thousand dollars in hundred-dollar bills and you decided to go away and begin life all over again, that you never were pregnant and the whole thing had been a scheme to try and force Harmon Haslett into matrimony."

"Why, the lying little . . ."

"Take it easy," Mason said. "It's necessary that you have this information quickly. Then we can discuss it after you know the facts.

"Maxine Edfield identified the detective as being you. She was about your height and complexion, and I had given her instructions as to how to walk and how to comport herself.

"The result was rather ludicrous. Maxine Edfield insisted that she was telling the truth. She also insisted that the detective was the woman she had known as Ellen Calvert, the woman who had confided in her.

"Everything blew sky high after Lovett's witness got herself in that trap.

"Now, then, you've walked into my office. If Garland and Dayton are still shadowing the office in the forlorn hope that you'll show up, they'll know from the description that they've hit pay dirt."

"Let them hit pay dirt," she said. "I'm going to come out in the open and fight."

"Fight for what?" Mason asked.

"Two million dollars for my son."

"Whoa, back up," Mason said. "That's an entirely different attitude from the one you had when you were here before."

"A woman has a right to change her mind."

"What brought about this change of heart on your part?" Mason asked.

She opened her purse, took from it another newspaper clipping.

"This article from *The Cloverville Gazette,* for one thing," she said.

Mason glanced at the headline: MANUFACTURER'S ESTATE VALUED AT TWO MILLION DOLLARS.

Mason raised his eyes from the headline. "You hadn't known this before?"

"No. I knew that Harmon Haslett was head of the business and virtually the sole stockholder, but I had no idea the business had grown so much in twenty years. It's evidently a real big company now."

"You understand what all this means?" Mason said. "If you try to claim that estate, you're going to be accused of fraud, you're going to be accused of perjury, your son is going to have his name dragged through the courts, and . . . He has no idea that you're his real mother?"

"He does now," she said. "I talked with him. I explained everything to him, and it was a lot easier than I had anticipated, because the woman he thought was his mother had made a couple of statements that had aroused his suspicions."

Mason regarded her thoughtfully. "You know," he said,

"you could be a very, very, very clever woman working in conspiracy with a young man of the proper age and making a very dramatic, carefully staged flimflam for the purpose of collecting a couple of million dollars."

"And you think I am an impostor?"

Mason said thoughtfully, "The way this thing has been engineered, the dramatic way the facts have been brought to light, I just don't know what to think. I'm only letting you know that I'm skeptical at the moment.

"Remember this: I'm not representing you any longer. Our relationship as attorney and client was terminated by you. Now you come to me with an entirely different plan of operation. I'm just telling you that I'm skeptical."

"I can't blame you, Mr. Mason," she said. "And I know now that I have acted like a fool. I should have taken everything into consideration."

"All right," Mason said, "let's have the real story; and, mind you, I am not asking you as a client. I am only asking you to tell me what you want me to do for the purpose of seeing whether I want to represent you.

"Now how much of what you told me was the truth?"

"Everything I told you was the truth," she said. "The only thing is I kept part of the truth from you."

"You did have a son?"

She said, "I came here just a little over twenty years ago. I was pregnant and desperate, but I had some money. I had what was left of the thousand dollars I had received —and since I had traveled in the cheapest way possible, I had a large part of that money.

"I couldn't take advantage of the office training I had had in the Haslett Company without giving it as a reference. Therefore, the only thing I had left was general housework and baby-sitting.

"I put an ad in the paper, and a Mrs. Baird answered the ad and asked me to call. I went out and had an interview. They were not very well fixed, but they had good credit and Mr. Baird had a steady job. The wife, Melinda Baird, was not at all well. They had no children. They looked like just an ordinary married couple.

"I went to work for them. Within a short time Mrs. Baird noticed my condition. I told her all about my trouble and told her that I would keep on working as long as I was able. Then I would go to a home for unwed mothers and have my child.

"She was very frank with me and very friendly. She asked me if I had considered the possibilities of an abortion, and I told her I had and that I wouldn't go for it.

"She didn't say anything more that day, but a couple of days later she talked with me and told me that she had had a long discussion with her husband—that they would like very much to adopt my baby but there were legal obstacles which made it impossible.

"So then Mrs. Baird came out with the proposition. She would tell her friends that she was pregnant. Mr. Baird would stay in Los Angeles and keep his job. But Mrs. Baird and I would go to San Francisco. When it came time for me to be confined, I would go to a San Francisco hospital under the name of Melinda Baird and have my child. The child would be registered as having been born to Melinda Baird and August Leroy Baird.

"That was all there need be to it. After a period of recuperation, we would return to Los Angeles. I could have a permanent job with them and they would bring up the child as their own. The only thing they asked was that I never let anyone—particularly the child—know the true state of affairs."

Mason studied the woman thoughtfully. "Why did you change your mind, and why do you come to me now?" he asked.

"Because of articles in the paper," she said, "showing that Harmon Haslett left an estate of over two million dollars. There are no heirs other than my son."

"You're not trying to get any for yourself?" Mason asked.

"I have no legal claim."

"Before, when I talked with you, you were very positive that you wanted your son to make his own way in the world, that you didn't want him to know that he had —as you expressed it, I believe—a heel for a father. Now there has been an abrupt change."

"I've been giving the matter a lot of thought. A few days ago I was thinking in terms of a live father and two or three hundred dollars a month as support money for my son. Now I am thinking in terms of a dead father and an estate of two million dollars for the boy."

"All of that," Mason said, "helps to make me skeptical."

She said, "It just happens that I can *prove* my story."

Mason sat forward in his chair. "Now that," he said, "would be interesting. How are you going to prove it? By the people who have been posing as the parents of . . . ?"

"No, they are both dead. They were killed in an automobile accident."

"How, then?"

"By a nurse at the hospital in San Francisco."

Mason said, "You mean you have a nurse who remembers what happened twenty years ago and who can testify to the circumstances surrounding one single birth out of all of the thousands which took place?"

"You're making it sound like something utterly incredible."

"Frankly, I think it is."

"Well, when you understand the circumstances, you'll realize that it's the most logical thing on earth."

"What are the circumstances?"

"This nurse had just started work in this hospital on the day that I was confined. Remember that I went into the hospital and took the name of Melinda Baird—and at that time, of course, I had to take the age of Melinda Baird, which I gave as twenty-nine. At the time I was only nineteen.

"Nobody noticed the discrepancy in ages except this one nurse, who happened to be checking the records and saw that my age was given as twenty-nine. Actually, Melinda Baird was thirty-one at the time, but we thought we could get by with a few years off on the official documents on the grounds that a woman always likes to make herself younger than she is.

"Anyway, this nurse thought there had been a mistake, and she came in to talk with me about it."

"What's her name?" Mason asked.

"Agnes Burlington."

"All right, she came in to see you before the child was born?"

"That's right."

"And asked you if you hadn't made a mistake in giving your age?"

"Yes."

"And what did you tell her?"

"I told her no—that I'd actually been born on the date I'd put in the records, that I was really older than I looked."

"What did she say?"

"She said, 'Bosh and nonsense,' and she asked me who I thought I was fooling, and finally I told her to give me a break and to just quit worrying about it.

"She was on her first assignment there at the hospital, and so she remembered the thing rather distinctly."

"That's no sign she could remember you personally," Mason said.

"Oh, but she does. I have talked with her."

"You've *talked* with her?"

"Yes."

"Where is she?"

"Here in Los Angeles. She has a nursing job here now."

"When did you talk with her?"

"Just a short time ago. That Agnes Burlington is diabolically clever. She had an idea of what was happening there in the hospital, so she just made a note of all of the records. Remember that I went there under the name of Melinda Baird and, of course, I gave the correct address at which Melinda Baird was living at the time. We had to do that in order to have the birth certificate and everything regular on its face.

"Well, Agnes Burlington bided her time, and then a couple of years ago she came to me and told me who she was, that she remembered me, and that she knew I had been posing as Melinda Baird and that the baby who was born and who was baptized Wight Baird was not the son of Melinda Baird and August Leroy Baird but was my illegitimate son."

"What did she want?" Mason asked.

"What do you think she wanted? Money. She was a shrewd, professional blackmailer. A nurse has lots and lots of opportunities for blackmail if she wants to use them, and this girl certainly wanted to use them."

"She's living here in Los Angeles now?"

"Yes."

"What's she doing?"

"She lives in a nice duplex house. She works when she feels like it. She drives a good car. She knows several places where she can go to get money when she needs it and . . ."

"How much has she hooked you for?" Mason asked.

"Not too much so far. She's reasonably modest in her demands and she's very, very plausible. She tells about how she needs a loan and things of that sort just to tide her over, a couple of hundred dollars now, and then a year later she'll be back for three hundred dollars, and always so nice about it."

"She said she remembered you?" Mason asked.

"Oh, yes—and actually I think she does—but she had one of those thirty-five-millimeter cameras and she got several pictures of me in the hospital—pictures I knew nothing about until she casually mentioned that she had them."

"Did she show them to you?"

"No."

"You don't think she's bluffing?"

"No, I think she has them."

Mason said thoughtfully, "So you've been paying black-mail to keep from having your past exposed and now, suddenly, you want to reverse the whole procedure?"

"Why not?" she asked. "The Bairds were killed in an automobile accident. Harmon Haslett is now dead. Wight is sole heir to a two-million-dollar estate and a big business.

"I have been wondering what I was going to do about Wight. Frankly, Mr. Mason, he's been just a little bit wild since the Bairds were killed in that automobile accident. They left a will giving him some money, and he's show-ing signs of—well, of being just a little bit wild.

"If he suddenly found himself the head of a great big business, if he found himself with plenty of money, he would steady down and assume the responsibility."

"You *hope* he would steady down and assume respon-sibility," Mason said. "He might go just the other way."

"No, not Wight," she said. "He's restless now because he doesn't have an assured position in life. Believe me, things were different when the Bairds were alive; but they died and he inherited just enough money—no, Mr. Mason, I've thought it all over. I've come to the conclu-sion that I reached a wrong decision when I first came to you and I want to change my entire position now."

"I see," Mason said; "and what do you want me to do now?"

"I want you to have Agnes sign an affidavit and—isn't there some proceeding by which you can get an affidavit or some sort of a legal document from a person who knows very important facts but who might die or turn up missing or something?"

"Where there is reason to believe a person is the only one who knows certain facts and the facts are vital to property interests, there *is* a procedure by which the testimony can be perpetuated."

"That's what I want done in this case."

"Your son is going under the name of Baird?"

"Yes. Wight Baird. One day when Melinda and August were both away and Wight was there in the house alone this woman came to call on him. She was very nice. She told him that she was one of the nurses in the hospital in San Francisco when he was born and that she attended his mother and that she wanted to see his mother. Evidently she was planning to blackmail the Bairds."

"This was the same nurse?"

"Oh, yes; she gave her name—Agnes Burlington."

"And then what happened?"

"She asked Wight about his mother—if his mother was a tall woman with what she called a commanding presence. And Wight laughed and said, 'No, she's medium height and inclined to be a little plump.' And one thing led to another and then this nurse went away."

Mason said, "You're not telling me the whole story. Let's have it all."

"All right," she said; "the nurse started blackmailing the Bairds. She hunted up Mr. Baird and told him who she was and told him that she had been one of the nurses when his son was born, and she made such thinly veiled statements about the mother's being a tall woman and how she'd talked with the mother and would remember her anywhere that when she wanted to borrow two hundred and fifty dollars Baird loaned it to her."

"Then what?"

"Then after a while she came back and borrowed two hundred and fifty more."

"How much altogether?"

"She put the bite on the Bairds for twelve hundred and fifty dollars in all."

"And where did that money come from? Did they pass it out willingly?"

"They paid it," Ellen said. "They were reluctant to pay it, but they had no choice."

"And during all of that time you were paying this nurse?"

"Yes, I was loaning her money."

"So now you want her to talk," Mason said musingly.

"Yes, I paid money to keep her from talking. Now it's just the other way. I *want* her to talk now. I'm going to want her to testify."

Mason said, "This could be one most ingenious and gigantic fraud."

"What do you mean?"

"You could have hatched this whole thing up after finding out there was a potential two-million-dollar estate to be had if a claimant . . . Look, Ellen, I'll talk with this nurse, but I'm going to be very, very skeptical—and I'll want to see proof—lots of proof."

"She can give you proof," Ellen Adair said.

Mason said, "I'll tell you what I'll do. We'll go call on

this Agnes Burlington. If I think she's telling the truth, I'll get an affidavit from her."

"And there's some way you can start proceedings so that you can perpetuate her testimony in case something should happen to her?" Ellen Adair asked.

"She's been around for twenty years," Mason said. "She'll probably be here a few years longer. But there *is* a procedure by which the testimony of a witness can be perpetuated."

"And we'll do that?"

Mason said, "The last time I talked with you, you dismissed me; you didn't want me as an attorney."

"The situation has changed since then. I have changed my mind about a lot of things."

"I'll say you have," Mason said. Then he asked abruptly, "What about Maxine Edfield?"

"What do you mean what about her?"

"How well did you know her?"

"Very well indeed."

"You asked her advice about things?"

"Yes; she was a few years older and I looked up to her."

"You double-dated with her?"

"Yes."

"You talked over your affair with Harmon Haslett?"

"Yes."

"You told her you were pregnant?"

"Yes."

"She knew about your getting the thousand dollars?"

"She was the only one who did know."

"Did you tell her that actually you weren't pregnant?"

"Of course not. I *was* pregnant; I was having morning

sickness. That's how Maxine happened to find out about it in the first place. She became terribly suspicious and started cross-examining me, and finally I had to tell her."

Mason said, "Now she swears that you told her you weren't pregnant, that it was all a racket to try and get Harmon Haslett to marry you."

"I know. Life hasn't been very kind to Maxine and someone has come along and dangled a lot of money in front of her. When there is two million dollars involved, Mr. Mason, you can expect almost anything to happen."

"You can say that again!" Mason said.

"Maxine is going to swear that it was all a part of a scheme for a shakedown?" Ellen asked.

"Not a shakedown; just that it was a part of a scheme to force Harmon Haslett into matrimony. She's already given her testimony. The only thing is that she identified the wrong person as being you. Now that put her in an embarrassing position when she made the statement. But, actually, it only means she made a wrong identification, which, after twenty years, is something anyone could do."

"You got her to identify the wrong person?"

"Well, I laid a trap for her and she walked into it," Mason said.

"And you'll go see Agnes Burlington with me?"

Mason sighed wearily. "All right," he said, "I'll go see her and listen to what she has to say. But I'll warn you of one thing. I'm not going to represent you until after I've satisfied myself about a lot of things."

"Why?"

"Because," Mason said, "a person accused of crime is entitled to a defense whether he's guilty or innocent. But a reputable lawyer doesn't want to get involved in a case of this kind where a client may be trying to put across a fraudulent claim."

"I can readily understand that, Mr. Mason. And if there were anything fraudulent about my claim, I wouldn't want you to represent me. I wouldn't even be coming forward.

"Even as it is, there was a while when I didn't want to set forth the claim. That is, not my claim but my son's claim. You can testify to that."

"I can remember what you *said*," Mason told her, "but it now seems your actions point in one direction, your words in another.

"As far as I'm concerned, you could be a very, very clever woman who pretended she was pregnant some twenty years ago, who tried to force Harmon Haslett into marriage, who failed in that attempt, who settled for a thousand dollars hush money, who came out here and got a job and worked her way up—but always with the idea that at the proper time she'd try and make a claim to the Haslett estate or make some kind of settlement.

"You looked around and found the Bairds, who were having a child at just about the date your child would have been due if your story had been correct.

"From that time on, you simply waited your time to cash in."

"But I couldn't do anything like that, Mr. Mason!"

"Why not?"

"It's completely, utterly foreign to my character! Can't you understand I've made good in the business world?

I've worked up until I'm chief buyer for French, Coleman and Swazey in the big department store. And then there's the testimony of this nurse."

"That testimony," Mason said, "will probably be the determining factor if it's genuine."

"But the minute you talk with her you'll find out that she's telling the truth. Of course, she won't like to admit the blackmail. But Wight can testify that she called at the house when the Bairds were out and asked for the Bairds and asked him to describe his mother. He was about twelve or thirteen at the time, and he'll remember it."

"You've talked it over with him?"

"No, but I'm quite sure he'll remember, because he told me all about it, and he told the Bairds."

"And she called on them?"

"Just on August Baird."

"And asked him for money?"

"Asked him for loans."

"And Baird paid off?"

"Yes, he had to."

"Did he have the money?"

"Yes."

"And he made the loans?"

"Yes."

"By check?"

"No, it was always handled on a cash basis."

"And August Baird is now dead?"

"Yes."

"And Melinda Baird is dead?"

"Yes, I told you they were killed in a car crash."

"Then we have your story," Mason said, "supported by absolutely nothing in the world except your uncorroborated statement and perhaps the testimony of this nurse. Opposed to that, we have the testimony of Maxine Edfield."

"Maxine is a liar!" Ellen said with feeling. "She has sold out!"

Mason said, "Well, I'll go and see this Agnes Burlington with you, but I warn you I'm going to give her a cross-examination.

"If this is all a lie, if you have concocted this story and intend to use Wight Baird as a pawn in the game, I warn you that I'm going to find out about it."

"And if you come to the conclusion that I'm not on the square?"

"I won't represent you," Mason said. "Right now you're not my client and I'm only considering the case. I'll go so far as to talk with Agnes Burlington with you and that's all!"

"When can you go?"

"When is it convenient?" Mason asked.

"Well, I think she's working days. We'll have to get her at night."

"This evening?" Mason asked.

"Why not?"

"You want to call her up and make an appointment?"

"No, that wouldn't be the smart thing to do. I think we should call on her and you should tell her that you're my attorney and ask her about the money she borrowed from August Baird and from me.

"Then she'll probably deny that she ever got any money from August, and I'll ask her about her conversation with Wight, and finally we'll get her to tell her story."

Mason shook his head. "I don't think I want to go at it that way, but I'll play it by ear. I'll meet this woman and talk with her."

"At eight o'clock tonight?"

"At eight o'clock tonight," Mason said. "Now you may be followed as soon as you leave this office. You made a mistake coming back here. You may have walked right into a trap. When you leave here . . . Did you come by car?"

"No, I took a bus."

"All right," Mason said. "Take a bus; ride on it until you come to a taxi which is parked at a stand where there is no other taxi. In other words, keep riding for an hour if you have to, until you come to a place where there is just one taxicab at the curb."

"And then?" she asked.

"Then," Mason said, "get out and take that taxicab. Make sure that there is no one following you with an automobile. When you feel that no one is following you, go home by a circuitous route.

"Now, then, tonight when I pick you up, Della Street and I will be out in Hollywood, driving along La Brea. We'll be driving south. At the corner of Beverly we'll bring the car into the curb at exactly eight o'clock.

"You be standing there at the curb. We'll open the door and let you in. Then we'll make sure that you aren't being followed, and then we'll go and see this nurse."

"But suppose somebody follows *you?*"

"They won't," Mason said. "I'll take precautions."

Ellen rose with queenly dignity, put her hand in Perry Mason's, and said, "Thank you very much, Mr. Mason. Thank you for your confidence and all you have done for me."

She turned and swept out of the office.

Della Street exchanged glances with Perry Mason. "Well?" she asked.

Mason shook his head. "This is one of those things," he said. "That woman can have engineered this whole thing so it looks like a convincing case. After all, we have her unsupported word, which is completely contradicted by the testimony of Maxine Edfield. And we *may* have the somewhat nebulous testimony of a nurse who, even according to our client, has been resorting to blackmail. And that's it!"

"And there's better than two million dollars involved," Della Street said.

"There's better than two million dollars involved. There are some very shrewd attorneys representing claimants on the other side, a couple of claimants who are viciously hostile, a private detective who is nobody's fool, and a troubleshooter who is just plain smart.

"If I have to go up against a combination of that sort, I want to be a lot more certain of the integrity of my client than I am of this woman with her somewhat condescending dignity and her air of utter assurance."

"Where do I meet you?" Della Street asked.

"You don't meet me," Mason said. "We go out and have dinner, then pick up our queenly client at La Brea and Beverly on the dot of eight o'clock."

Chapter Nine

PROMPTLY at eight o'clock Mason pulled his car into the La Brea curb, and immediately Ellen Adair detached herself from the shadows, crossed the sidewalk and jumped into the car.

"You came by cab?" Mason asked.

"That's right."

"Were you followed?"

"Absolutely not."

"All right," Mason told her; "now where do we go?"

"Keep on down La Brea for a ways, then we turn to the right. I haven't been to this place for six months, but I think I remember the way."

"What sort of a place is it?"

"It's a duplex bungalow. Agnes Burlington has the place on the west. It's a cute little place with a lawn and a gravel driveway."

"When were you there last?"

"I guess it's all of six months ago."

"How did you happen to go there?"

"I went there to try and buy Agnes Burlington's silence. At that time I wanted her to keep quiet."

"You paid her money?"

"I made her a loan."

"Now," Mason said, "you want her to start talking. Has it ever occurred to you she may not be receptive to your proposition?"

"You mean that she'll want more money?"

"Yes."

"You mean first I pay her *not* to talk and now I pay her to get her to talk."

"You don't pay her," Mason said. "You can't afford to."

"Why not?"

"Because the other side would claim that was suborning perjury. In a case of this kind, you can't afford to put yourself in the position of paying a witness to testify."

"What can we do?"

"If she's reluctant," Mason said, "we might decoy her into believing that you still don't want her to talk and get her to make threats to tell the truth."

"What good will that do?"

"We'd get her to repeat the threats under such circumstances that there'd be a tape recorder concealed in some advantageous place where we can record the entire conversation."

"Turn to the right here," Ellen Adair said. And then, after Mason had made the turn, she added, "That's really a good idea. I think perhaps we can work that with her— if she's reluctant. But I think she'll tell her story. She'll do quite a bit of talking now."

Mason drove several blocks, then Ellen said, "Turn to the right again here. Go two blocks, then . . . No, wait a minute, I'm confused. You go three blocks and then turn to the left, and it's about midway down the block. Let's see, it's—there it is, Mr. Mason. That house over there on the right—the duplex house. Agnes Burlington's side of the house is the one on the west."

Mason eased the car in to the curb.

"You can drive right on up the driveway," she said.

Mason said, "That driveway looks soft. You can see where someone has been in there and left deep tracks. The way the lawn is sloped, water from the grass seeps down into the driveway and . . ."

"But go in there anyway; get the car off the road!"

Mason said, "I think it's too soft, Ellen. This is a heavy car."

"It has big tires," she said.

"But what do we gain?" Mason asked. "We'll park here at the curb. I don't like to go into someone's driveway and park when we're going to call on a business matter."

"Oh, she'll understand."

"No, we're all right where we are," Mason said in a tone of finality, opening the door on the driver's side, then crossing behind the car to open the door for Della Street and then Ellen Adair.

They walked up a cement walk which led to a porch with two front doors, one on the left and one on the right.

Mason pressed the bell button on the door on the left.

There was no sound of motion from within the house, only the sound of the bell jangling.

"She doesn't seem to be home," Ellen said.

"Oh, I think probably she's home," Mason said. "The lights are all on. She may be busy for the moment."

"Perhaps the bell didn't ring."

"No, I could hear it inside the house," Della Street said.

Once more Mason pressed the button, and again from the interior of the house was the unechoing sound of the bell.

"Well," Mason said, "I suggest we go back to the car and wait five or ten minutes and try again. After all, she may be taking a shower."

"Perhaps she's in the kitchen and can't hear the bell. She might have a dishwasher running or perhaps she's got a clothes-washing machine going and . . . Why not go around to the back and take a look?" Ellen asked.

Mason said, "The other side of the house is dark—the other unit of the duplex. The people there are probably out, but I don't like to go wandering around at the back of houses."

Mason tried the bell button twice more, then moved over a few feet along the porch to press his forehead against the cold glass of the windowpane.

"See anything?" Della Street asked.

"I can see the interior of the living room," Mason said, "through a half-inch crack where the drapes aren't pulled tightly together. I can see . . . Hold everything!"

"What is it?" Della Street asked.

Mason said, "I can see the foot of a woman."

"What's she doing?" Della Street asked.

"Nothing," Mason said. "The foot is in another room, which may be a bedroom. The toe is pointed straight up. It shows through the crack in the door."

"Oh, good lord!" Ellen said. "If anything's happened to her, I . . . Let me see."

She moved over to stand beside the lawyer, pressing her hands against the glass in order to form a shield for her eyes, cutting out the rays of light which might come in at the sides.

Mason said, "That foot looks strangely still. Evidently a woman is lying on the floor. Try the front door, Della. See if it's locked. Knock at the same time you press the bell button."

"She's unconscious," Ellen said. "She isn't moving an inch."

"The front door's locked," Della Street reported.

Mason said, "I think we'd better call the police."

"No, no, no!" Ellen protested. "Not until we've tried to find out what it's all about. If she's just drunk or drugged or something, we've simply got to get her testimony before anyone else can get to her. Can't you understand what it means to me to have her get on the stand and tell the truth?"

Mason hesitated.

Ellen Adair said, "If she's drunk and passed out and . . ."

"It's early for her to have passed out from drinking," Mason said. "All right, let's go around to the back of the house and try the back door. And, incidentally, we'll see if there's another window we can peep in and perhaps get a better view."

The lawyer walked down the front steps, started across the lawn for the driveway, paused after taking a couple of steps, and said, "This soil is plenty soft. Somebody's been sprinkling the lawn quite heavily. There's an underground irrigation system which is still running at a trickle. It's been on for some time."

"Let's go around the other way, circling around the other side of the duplex," Ellen said.

"That puts us in the position of being trespassers," Mason observed, "but we may as well go the whole way now we've started."

He led the way across the lawn on the other side of the duplex bungalow, around to the back, over to the west side of the duplex, and climbed a short flight of steps to a service porch and said, "Oh-oh, the door's open a crack. I think we can get in here."

"Well?" Ellen asked as Mason hesitated.

Mason paused a moment, then said, "All three of us keep together. Be careful not to touch anything. Be sure that we call out as soon as we get the door open."

Mason pushed the back door open. "Anybody home?" he called in a loud voice. Then, as there was a silence, the lawyer shouted, "Hello! Miss Burlington!"

There was no answer.

The lawyer moved across the kitchen and into a lighted living room, turned to the right into a bedroom in which drapes were drawn over the windows and electric lights were turned on, and then suddenly froze into rigid immobility.

"All right," Mason said, "this is it. Keep back."

The woman who was lying on the floor was perhaps forty-two or forty-three years of age, with dark hair streaming out over the floor, part of the ends matted in a pool of dried blood.

She was wearing shoes, stockings, a garter girdle, and a bra.

The lawyer said to the two women, "Keep back and don't touch anything!"

Mason stepped gingerly forward, bent over the body, and picked up a limp, cold arm.

The lawyer held the wrist for a moment, then let the arm drop back.

"She's been dead for some time," he said. "Rigor mortis has formed and disappeared. There's postmortem lividity. It's a job for the police."

Ellen Adair pushed past Della Street, grabbed Perry Mason by the arm. "Oh, Mr. Mason, do something! For heaven's sake, we can't take a beating in this thing!"

Mason said, "Get back out of the way. You can't bring a person back to life just because you want her testimony."

"Oh, my God! This is terrible!" Ellen said, letting go of Mason's arm, turning toward the door, stumbling over the body, trying to catch her balance, grabbing hold of the dresser. Then as she saw her feet were touching the legs of the dead woman she started screaming.

Mason grabbed her, said to Della Street, "Get her out of here! Don't let her touch anything, Della!"

The lawyer swung Ellen Adair toward Della Street, but Ellen once more stumbled, grabbed the side of the door, then hung onto Della Street, crying and moaning.

"I think she's going to have hysterics," Della Street said.

"She can't have hysterics," Mason said. "I want to take a quick look, but I don't want to touch anything. We can't . . . Watch her, Della!"

"Let me out of here!" Ellen screamed, breaking away

from Della and making a stumbling, zigzag, flying course for the front door, which she opened.

Della Street said to Mason, "She's hysterical. We can't let her go running around . . ."

Mason sprinted after Ellen Adair, caught her at the foot of the front steps, said, "Sit down and control yourself!"

Ellen started to scream. The lawyer clapped his hand over her mouth, pulled her down on the cement steps.

"Sit down!" he repeated.

She looked at him with wide, panic-stricken eyes and once more tried to scream.

Mason said, "Della, there's a service station three blocks down the street with a telephone. Get to it and call the police, then come back here. I'll hold Ellen until you can get back."

The lawyer turned to the hysterical woman.

"Now shut up!" he said. "Don't make a lot of commotion and attract the attention of everyone in the neighborhood. We're dealing with what is, in all probability, a murder, and I want you to keep your head."

Della Street hurried down the short stretch of cement walk, jumped in the car, turned on the motor, and shot away from the curb.

Mason said to Ellen, "Now I'm going to take my hand away and I don't want you screaming. The police are going to come here, and I don't want you to tell the police *why* we were calling on Agnes Burlington. I particularly don't want you to say anything about ever at any time having paid Agnes Burlington any money to keep quiet about anything. Do you understand?"

The wide, panic-stricken eyes searched Mason's face. The lawyer removed his hand from Ellen Adair's mouth.

"Do you understand?" Mason said. "Let me do the talking!"

Ellen Adair took a deep breath. "This is such a shock!" she said; then her body stiffened. "I think I'm going to faint."

Mason pushed her shoulders forward. "Put your head down between your knees," he said.

Ellen lurched against Mason.

The lawyer pushed on her shoulders, guided her head down to her knees.

"Sit there, Ellen. Try not to think about what you've seen. Think about what we are going to have to do now."

Ellen's body became limp.

Mason supported it for a matter of a full minute before, gradually, the muscles responded. Ellen breathed a tremulous breath, raised herself, looked at Mason. Then her eyes became wide with panic once more.

"Easy," Mason said. "The police will be coming any minute now. You've got to pull yourself together! Remember the police can't keep information of this sort confidential. They'll be reporting that the body was discovered by Perry Mason, his secretary and a client. The newspaper reporters will pick it up. They'll want to know who you are; they'll want to know what your business with me is; they'll find out all about the Cloverville background. Maxine will come forward with her story. The police will search the premises here. Maybe Agnes kept a diary. They'll get the names of her friends. Maybe Agnes talked. She probably has a boyfriend somewhere. She may have confided in him at length.

"We've got to keep ourselves in such a position that we can be prepared no matter which way the cat jumps. You've too much at stake to go feminine on me now. Get yourself together!"

Ellen took a deep breath. "I'm sorry," she mumbled.

Mason said, "Here comes a car and . . . it's stopping . . . It's Della."

Della Street had pulled the car into the curb and just opened the door to disembark when a police car swung around the corner, glided to the curb. A red spotlight illuminated Della Street. An officer said, "Hold it, lady!"

Della froze.

Mason said, "Now sit tight, Ellen," and arose from the step.

"This way, Officer," Mason called.

An officer jumped from the car, came toward the sound of Mason's voice.

"Who are you?" he asked.

"Perry Mason," the lawyer said.

"Who's the girl?"

Mason, walking rapidly toward the officer so he could keep his voice low, said, "She's my secretary."

"What's the trouble?"

"There's a body in the house."

"How do you know?"

"We were in there."

"How did you get in?"

"Through the back door."

"What were you doing prowling around the back door?"

Mason said, "We had reason to believe there was somebody home. We rang the doorbell and got no answer. I looked through the front window and could see a woman's foot. We went around to the back of the house. The back door was unlocked; in fact, it was standing slightly ajar —open about half an inch, I would say. We went in."

"Touch anything?" the officer asked.

"I'm afraid my client touched a few things. She became hysterical and started running through the house. She stumbled over furniture. I grabbed her, got her out here into the open air, and sent my secretary to call you."

"Where did you have your car parked?"

"At the curb," Mason said. "The front lawn and the driveway are rather soft. I think there's an automatic sprinkler system which has been turned on low and has been left running for some time. I felt the body to see if there was any sign of life. The flesh is cold, lifeless and limp, which means that rigor mortis has not only formed but has had time to disappear. The soft lawn indicates the irrigation system has been on for some time. Lights are on inside the house, and I have an idea they've been on all day and probably all night last night."

"We'll take a look," the officer said. He turned to his partner. "Call Homicide." He said to Mason, "Get in your car and stay there. Don't go away. Who's the woman on the steps?"

"Come here, Ellen," Mason said.

Ellen Adair got up and walked slowly but steadily toward the officer.

Mason said, "This is my client. She's emotional and unstrung. She's a responsible businesswoman; her name is Ellen Adair, and she's head buyer for French, Coleman and Swazey, the big department store."

"All right," the officer said. "The three of you get in your car. I'll just take a look at your driver's license, Mr. Mason, if you don't mind."

Mason showed the officer his driver's license.

The man in the car reported, "Homicide is on its way out here. We're supposed to cover the premises front and back."

"O.K., I'll take the back," the first officer said. "You watch the front. And keep an eye on these people. This is Perry Mason, the lawyer."

"Don't start around the back of the house over the lawn," Mason said, "or the driveway. The lawn is mushy and some of the water has run into the driveway. Go around the side of the other duplex. That's the way we went."

"Thanks," the officer told him. Then he asked, "How did you know the lawn is soft if you didn't go around that way?"

"I just took two steps," the lawyer said.

"I see," the officer announced noncommittally, and, sending the beam of a flashlight in front of him, walked around the side of the duplex on the east to take up a station at the rear of the house.

The officer in the car said, "You three people may just as well get in your parked automobile and stay there until Homicide comes."

Chapter Ten

LIEUTENANT TRAGG of Homicide leaned against the door on the driver's side of Mason's automobile.

"How did it happen you discovered the body?" Tragg asked.

"We went to call on Agnes Burlington. We rang the doorbell; we got no answer. The lights were on. I looked through the window; I saw a woman's foot. We went around the back of the duplex house and I saw the back door on the west unit was open a small crack."

"So you pushed the door open and went in?"

"Right."

"Why didn't you telephone for the police the minute you saw the woman's foot?"

Mason laughed. "I didn't want to take an ordinary drunk case where a woman had had too many cocktails and had passed out and magnify it into something that would make the newspapers . . . and involve me in a damage suit."

Tragg said, "For your private information, Mason, we don't like lawyers who go around discovering bodies. You've done it before—too often."

Mason said, "I'm a lawyer who gets out on the firing line. I can't sit in an office and wait for a case to develop."

"All right, all right," Tragg said; "we've been over this before. You're a lawyer who gets out on the firing line; you can't sit in an office and wait for a case to develop. Now, then, what was it you couldn't wait to have develop in this case?"

Mason said, "I have reason to believe Agnes Burlington was a witness in a case which is of some importance to a client of mine."

"What kind of a case?"

"That," Mason said, "I can't discuss."

"And what did you think Agnes Burlington was going to testify to?"

"Again, that's something I can't discuss."

"Playing cozy and secretive all the time, aren't you, Mason?"

Mason said, "I try to protect the interests of my clients."

"All right," Tragg said, "you went in. You found the body. You touched it?"

"Yes."

"Why?"

"To see if she was merely unconscious."

"The evidence indicates she had been dead for some time. You didn't notice that the blood was all dried?"

"I noticed it," Mason said. "But if the woman was alive, I was going to do everything I could to give her help."

"As soon as you touched her you knew that she was dead?"

"Yes—and had been dead for some time."

"You ever talked with this Agnes Burlington before?"

"No, I hadn't."

"What do you know about her?"

"She was a nurse."

Tragg looked across the steering wheel into Ellen Adair's eyes. "This woman is your client?" he asked.

"Right," Mason said. "This is my client."

"And you say she's a responsible businesswoman?"

"She's head buyer for the big department store of French, Coleman and Swazey."

Tragg looked past Ellen Adair to Della Street and smiled. "And we know all about the incomparable Della Street, your secretary.

"All right," Tragg said; "let's hear from this young woman. What's your name?"

"Ellen Adair."

"Ellen Adair is hardly in a position to make a statement," Mason said. "She's my client."

"Stop her any time you want her to stop talking," Tragg said, smiling. "Go ahead; let's hear what you have to say."

Ellen Adair said, "I came here with Mr. Mason and Miss Street. We found the woman dead and promptly called the police."

"Did you touch anything?"

"We left things just as we found them."

"Why did you come here?"

Mason shook his head and smiled. "We're getting into the matters I prefer not to discuss at this time."

Tragg said, "You just came in here, found the dead woman, and called the police?" His eyes were studying Ellen Adair's face.

"Yes," she said.

"All right," Tragg announced; "you folks can leave now. We know where to reach you if we want you."

"Thanks," Mason said.

"Not at all," Tragg said with exaggerated courtesy. "It's a real pleasure to cooperate with people who are so anxious to cooperate with us."

Chapter Eleven

"Is that all there is to it?" Ellen Adair asked in a surprised tone of voice as Lieutenant Tragg turned back toward the duplex house and Mason started the motor.

"That *isn't* all there is to it," Mason said. "This is only the very start."

"But he didn't question me at all about what I knew about the dead woman or why we were here or . . ."

"Because," Mason said, "he felt certain that I wouldn't let you answer all the questions he asked and, if you did answer them, he had no way of knowing if you were lying."

"What do you mean by that?"

"Up to this point," Mason said, "Lieutenant Tragg knows very little more about the murder as such than we do.

"We can estimate the time of death, but we have to rely on rigor mortis, on lights that have been left on, on a sprinkling system which has been turned down very low and left running for some time.

"Probably Agnes Burlington was killed some twenty-four hours earlier.

"But rigor mortis is one of the most deceiving methods of determining the time of death. Sometimes rigor mortis is virtually instantaneous; sometimes it is very slow in forming.

"There are other methods of determining the time of death—body temperature, the time when food was ingested, the condition of the food in the stomach and intestines, and all that.

"Tragg knows that we are all responsible people. We aren't going to try to duck out of any inquiry. He knows that I have told him the truth, but he isn't certain that I've told him *all* the truth. In fact, he is almost certain that I have withheld certain vital pieces of information, such as why we were anxious to interview Agnes Burlington, what the case is all about, why you are my client, and all the rest of it."

"I am your client, am I not?" she asked as Mason turned the car back onto the boulevard.

"I suppose so," the lawyer said wearily. "I'm stuck with you now. You didn't want me to represent you anymore, then you came back in a panic. Why did you come back in a panic, Ellen?"

"I didn't come back in a panic. I got to thinking things over and decided that if there was two million dollars involved, there was going to be enough publicity so I couldn't escape it. I felt that they would find me and I felt that they'd find Agnes Burlington, and then they'd find Wight and . . . well, I decided that it was about time for me to come out in the open and that Wight was going to have to adjust himself sooner or later to the realities of the situation.

"I thought it would be a lot easier on him to adjust to the realities if he had two million dollars."

"And so you came back to me."

"So I came back to you," she said.

Mason drove silently for several blocks, then said, "You're a pretty cool sort of a customer, Ellen."

"I'm intensely human," she said, "but I try to control myself."

"That's what I'm getting at," Mason said. "You have a certain amount of control. Right now you're just as cool as a cucumber."

"Is there any reason why I shouldn't be?"

"You were hysterical a short time ago."

"I got over the hysteria. And, of course, a sudden emotional storm like that has the tendency to clear the atmosphere."

"And leave you cool, calm and collected."

"Well, a lot calmer than I was when we discovered the body."

Mason said, "It was the way you acted when we discovered the body that was just a little out of character. I told you not to touch anything. You went stumbling around, falling over things in general, falling over the body in particular, grasping at the surface of the dresser —and then you got up and broke away from Della Street and stumbled into the wall and pushed yourself back with your hands, zigzagged across the room, ran into the wall two or three times, put your hands all over the inside of the front door, and dashed out.

"Prior to that time, when I'd been looking in the windows, you made it a point to come over and stand beside me and cup your hands so that you could see through the window."

"Well," she asked, "is there anything wrong with all that?"

"You left fingerprints all over the place," Mason said.

"I'm sorry."

"You may be even more sorry," Mason told her. "Tragg is not going to like that. He'll find altogether too many of your fingerprints."

"Well, I don't know whether Tragg will understand or not. But, after all, he's a veteran police officer and he must have seen women go to pieces before.

"After all, Mr. Mason, a woman is not a cold, reasoning machine. She relies on intuition as much as logic, and she is at times high-strung and temperamental."

"I know, I know," Mason said. "But a thought keeps circulating through my mind, and I'm wondering if it will occur to Lieutenant Tragg."

"What thought?" she asked.

"That you knew Agnes Burlington was dead when you came to my office the second time."

"Why, Mr. Mason!" she exclaimed. "Why . . . why, I never heard anything like that in all my life! You are accusing me of deception and duplicity!" Her voice trailed into indignant silence.

"I'm not accusing you of anything," Mason said. "I'm asking you a question. Did you know Agnes Burlington was dead when you came to my office?"

"Of course not!"

Mason said, "I'm going to let you do a little thinking, Ellen. If you had been at that house before, if you knew that Agnes Burlington was lying there dead, you're in just as much trouble as though you had gone to that house with a gun, pulled the trigger, and sent the fatal bullet into Agnes Burlington's body."

"Well, I told you I didn't know anything about it. I didn't have any idea that she was dead. I thought we'd find her alive and well and you could talk with her."

Mason said thoughtfully, "I wonder." Then suddenly he said, "In the driveway, Ellen, there were tracks. The water had seeped down through the sloping lawn onto the driveway."

"Well?" she asked.

"You seemed unduly anxious to get me to put my car in the driveway," Mason said. "In fact, you were quite insistent that I should go up that muddy driveway."

"I thought it would be better if we parked the car in the driveway and . . ."

"Why?"

"Why, because it . . . well, I don't know. It just seemed to me to be the thing to do."

"I am wondering," Mason said, "if you wanted me to use my car to obliterate the tracks which had been left in that muddy driveway. I am wondering if *you* had driven out to the house earlier in the day and had left your car parked in the driveway; if you had started across to the front door, found that the lawn was soft, that your feet were bogging down in the soft soil, and so had gone back to the driveway, gone around to the back door, knocked at the back door, found that it was open, gone in, and found Agnes Burlington's body.

"I am wondering if you started looking around a little bit before you did anything, perhaps looking to see if she had left a diary or some papers, and, in that way, left your fingerprints in the house.

"Then I am wondering if, when you decided that you had to get yourself out of a jam, you didn't come to me and get me to go out to the house, planning for me to discover the body and having it all planned in advance that you could have a case of hysterics and leave your fingerprints all over the place so that I could tell Lieutenant Tragg what had happened, in order to explain your fingerprints."

"Mr. Mason," she said with cold dignity, "I think, under those circumstances, you are hardly in a position to act as my attorney!"

"Anytime you want out of the relationship," Mason said, "you don't need to hesitate for a minute. But I'm warning you that if what I said is correct, you're facing a first-degree murder trial. Don't kid yourself for a minute that anything as simple as your plot will fool Lieutenant Tragg for more than twenty-four hours. Now think it over."

Ellen Adair was silent.

"Well?" Mason asked. "What about it? What's happened to the cold, dignified indignation?"

Suddenly Ellen Adair slumped over against Della Street's shoulder.

"It's true," she said.

Mason muttered an exclamation under his breath, abruptly turned the wheel of the car.

"Where are we going now?" Ellen Adair asked.

"To some place where no one can find us until I've hammered the real truth out of you," Mason said.

Chapter Twelve

"I've already told you the truth," Ellen said. "You don't need to go anywhere."

"You little fool!" Mason said. "You've got yourself in a mess, and now you've dragged me in it with you!

"Don't make the mistake of underestimating the police. They'll find tire tracks outlined as plain as can be in that mud in the driveway. They'll be wondering what we were doing out there. They have your name and address from your driver's license. They'll find your car. They'll take impressions of your tires. They'll make a moulage of the tracks in the driveway. They'll come to the conclusion that you went out there and killed Agnes Burlington and then came to me telling me what you'd done and that I went out there with you to remove some evidence that would be incriminating and then, after we had the evidence removed, we notified the police.

"Lieutenant Tragg will put out a bulletin to pick us up for questioning."

"I could change my tires on the car before they could . . ."

"Don't kid yourself!" Mason interrupted. "You'd simply be buying yourself a one-way ticket to prison. What did you do with the gun?"

"What gun?"

"I think she had been shot. There could have been a gun by the body."

"There wasn't any gun."

The lawyer turned the car from the boulevard sharply to the left, drove to a beach motel, rented two adjoining rooms, put Della Street and Ellen Adair in one room, and then opened the connecting door.

"All right," he said, "now we'll sit down here and have an hour or so to talk before we have to face the music."

Ellen Adair said, "I guess I shouldn't have tried to deceive you. I . . ."

"That," Mason said, "is the understatement of the week! Now, then, what I want to know is this: *did* you kill Agnes Burlington?"

"Good heavens, Mr. Mason, I couldn't kill anyone! No, I didn't kill her!"

"When did you go out there?"

"A little after noon."

"What did you find?"

"I found things just as we saw them."

"Now I want the truth," Mason said. "Was there any gun lying around?"

"No, there was no gun."

"What did you do?"

"I got in a panic, and then I wondered what sort of papers she might have left around and I gave a quick look."

"Did you find any?"

"There was a diary."

"What did you do with it?"

"I didn't have time to read it. I just grabbed it, and then I got out of there. Then I got to thinking what a horrible thing I had done and . . ."

"Did you read any of the diary?"

"Yes. I read a good deal of it."

"What did it show?"

"I think it was kept in some sort of code, because she would say at times, 'I telephoned so-and-so for a date'; then she would say, 'I had a date with so-and-so'; and then she would say, 'I had a satisfactory date with so-and-so,' and would underline the 'satisfactory.' "

"Anybody in there that you know?" Mason asked.

She said, "Not names. She used initials most of the time. But there was one thing in there that bothered me terribly."

"What?"

"There was a note about three months ago saying, 'I subscribed to *The Cloverville Gazette*.' "

"Where is that diary now?"

"I hid it."

"Where?"

"Where no one will ever find it."

"Don't be too sure," Mason said. "The police are very, very thorough."

"And I," she said, "am very, very ingenious."

"You," Mason told her, "are a babe in the woods. You caught me with my guard down. If it hadn't been for that,

I'd have given you enough cross-examination about what caused your sudden change of heart to have smelled a mouse.

"Now, then, I've gone out there with you. If the officers can prove that that's your second trip out there, that you had already been out and found her dead—if they can prove that you took that diary, you're going to be convicted of murder."

"What can I do?" she asked.

"Right now," Mason said, "you can't do anything except keep quiet. You can't afford to give the officers the time of day. If they ask you questions, you've got to tell them that you're not answering any questions on the advice of counsel."

"But won't that make me look guilty?"

"You start in answering questions," Mason said, "and before you get done you'll look like a murderess. They'll catch you in a lie. They'll spring the trap on you and have you dead to rights."

"But if I don't say anything, they'll convict me anyway," she said.

"If you keep quiet, you stand a fighting chance," Mason told her. "They'll *think* you're guilty. They'll arrest you and try you for first-degree murder. But they've got to prove their case, and they have to prove it beyond all reasonable doubt.

"Now *somebody* murdered Agnes Burlington. That someone murdered her for a reason.

"You're going to have to reconcile yourself to going to trial. You're going to have to take the chance of being convicted. The only thing that will stand between you and a sure conviction is getting the breaks, watching the evidence, cross-examining witnesses, searching for a weak point in the prosecution's case—then, when we find that weak point, bearing down hard on it and turning it into a reasonable doubt in the minds of the jurors.

"So now, while we have the time, we've got to run down every possible lead that we can in order to find something that we can translate into a reasonable doubt. The police are going to be uncovering evidence, and they're not going to share that evidence with us until they have to. They certainly aren't going to take us into their confidence."

"Do you," she asked, "want that diary?"

Mason said, "I'm an officer of the court. I couldn't suppress evidence. I couldn't have a diary in my possession for ten seconds without telling the police that I had it.

"On the other hand, as an officer of the court, I am obligated to protect your confidences. You tell me that you have the diary. I can *advise* you to surrender that diary to the police. But if you don't choose to follow my advice, there's nothing I can do about it except keep quiet. I have a professional obligation to respect your confidence.

"Now, then, what about your son?"

"What do you mean?"

"The officers are going to find out about him. What kind of an impression will he make?"

"A very fine impression, Mr. Mason. He's a nice, well-mannered young man. He . . ."

"Where's he living?"

"He's living in the old Baird home. After Melinda and August were killed he inherited all their property, and he has been living on there in the house."

"O.K.," Mason said, getting up with an air of finality, "we're going to go call on your son, and let's hope we beat the police to it."

Mason nodded to Della Street. "Let's go."

Chapter Thirteen

ELLEN ADAIR, who had been giving Mason driving directions, said, "Turn to the right at this next corner, and it's the house in the middle of the block."

"You think your son will be home?" the lawyer asked.

"He should be."

"And he knows you as . . ."

"He knows the truth now, but for years he thought I was just a friend of the family, related in some way to the Bairds. He never asked too much about details. He took the relationship for granted and called me 'Aunt Ellen.'"

"All right," Mason said, "let's hope he's home."

"He will be. He'll be studying. He has an examination coming up and . . . Here's the place."

The lawyer slid the car beside the curb.

"All right, let's go. Remember—you say absolutely nothing at any time that would indicate you had been to see Agnes Burlington twice today. You are never, under any circumstances, to tell any human being the things you have told us. All right, now; let's go up and take a look at this boy."

They left the car, walked up the cement walk and past the well-kept lawn.

"Who does the work here?" Mason asked. "Your son?"

"I think he hires it done. There's a gardener. There's a lot of yard work, you know, and, after all, Wight is busy with his studies."

Ellen Adair pushed her thumb against the bell button, giving a series of short, sharp rings, then a long ring, then two short rings.

She smiled at Mason. "We have a code so he'll know who's at the door."

They waited for some fifteen seconds and then Ellen Adair said, "Why, that's strange. He must be home. His car is in the driveway."

"That his car?" Mason asked, indicating a low-slung sports car.

"Yes."

"That's an expensive car," Mason observed.

"He is very modern, Mr. Mason, and—well, the Bairds left him this money. He . . . I can't understand what's delaying him."

She pressed the button again, a series of short, sharp rings, then a long ring and a couple of short rings.

Della Street exchanged glances with Perry Mason.

Abruptly from the back of the house a man's voice called, "Whoo-hoo, I'm coming," and then a few moments later the door was swung open and a well-built, good-looking young man said, "Aunt Ellen—Mom! What brings you here at this time of night?"

Ellen Adair said, "Wight, I want you to meet Perry Mason, the famous attorney; and this is Della Street, his confidential secretary."

Wight Baird regarded his visitors with openmouthed amazement. "Gosh," he said, "the famous lawyer! What's all *this* about?"

Ellen said, "We're coming in, Wight. We have to talk with you about a matter of great importance."

"Is all this about the will?" Wight asked.

"Yes."

"Gee, Mom, is Mr. Mason going to be on our side?"

"He's going to be on our side," Ellen said, "but there are lots of complications."

"I'll bet," Wight said. "You get to kicking a couple of million bucks around and there'll be *lots* of complications. Come on in."

He led the way into a living room.

"You were quite a while answering the bell," Ellen said.

Wight said, "I called out just as soon as you rang the bell."

"Then you didn't hear it the first time?"

"You mean you rang twice?"

"Yes."

"Gosh, no, Aunt Ellen—Mom—I didn't hear it the first time."

The sound of a motor starting came from the driveway.

Wight said, somewhat hastily, "I'm cramming for an exam. I've been holding my nose to the grindstone all afternoon and evening. I'm about all in. Forgive me if I seem a little dopey. What's new, Aunt—Mom? Why are you coming here at this hour of the night with Mr. Mason and his secretary?"

Ellen said, "There was a witness that we called on—a rather mature woman who had some information that would have been of value. We went to call on her. Mr. Mason wanted to talk with her."

"Yeah, sure," Wight said. "That's a smart move. Let's get the evidence rounded up."

"We got there too late," Ellen said. "She was dead."

"Dead!"

"That's right."

"How come?"

"She had evidently been murdered," Mason said.

"Murdered!" Wight exclaimed. "Say, what are you doing—trying to put one over on me? You don't . . . good lord!"

Ellen said, "Mr. Mason feels that we may be questioned in some detail, and I wanted to come to you and explain the situation, and Mr. Mason wanted to talk with you."

"Who was this jane?" Wight asked. "Anybody I know?"

"No one you know," Ellen said. "She had been a nurse in San Francisco at the time you were born, and—"

"Hey, wait a minute," Wight interrupted. "You don't, by any chance, mean Agnes Burlington, do you?"

"Agnes Burlington!" his mother exclaimed. "Do you know her?"

"Why, sure."

"How did you meet her?" Mason asked.

"She hunted me up," Wight said.

"How long ago?"

"The first time was just after the Bairds died. She told me that I wasn't the real son of August Baird, that Mrs. Baird had put up a job on him and palmed me off as his son.

"She said that if the facts were known I'd be penniless. She said that would be a great shame because it wasn't my fault. She told me then that you were my real mother and a lot of stuff . . ."

"How much did you agree to pay her?" Mason asked.

"Ten per cent of whatever I inherited from the Bairds."

"Why, Wight! You never told me about this!" Ellen exclaimed.

"She said not to. She told me not to tell anyone. She warned me against telling you in particular. She said I'd lose everything."

"You paid her the ten per cent?" Mason asked.

"Yes."

"When did you next see her after that?" Mason asked.

"Just a couple of days ago."

"What did she want?"

"She told me that it might be possible I could inherit a very substantial sum of money and asked me what it would be worth to me percentage-wise if . . ."

"Why, Wight, you should have told me," Ellen Adair said.

"Well, to tell you the truth, Mom, I never had much of a chance. I only see you briefly once in a while, and I thought this Burlington dame was talking through her hat, but I told her to go get me some money and she could have her percentage of it."

"Did she say how much money?" Mason asked.

"She said quite a large sum of money."

"You knew she had been a nurse in San Francisco?"

"That's right. That first time she told me that she had been a nurse in San Francisco and she told me that she attended my mother when I was born—and that my parents weren't the Bairds at all. I let her do the talking. I didn't say very much."

"You're living here in this house alone?" Mason asked.

"That's right. A woman comes in and keeps things clean; she does the dishes and makes the bed."

"She comes in every day?"

"Yes."

"You've been in all day?" Mason asked.

"That's right—had my nose buried in books."

"Ellen Adair here has a key to the place?" Mason asked.

"Why, yes, sure, she has a key. She always rings the code signal when she comes, but she has a key and could get in if she wanted to."

"If she had something she wanted to hide, is there any place here where she could leave it?"

"Dozens of places," Wight said.

"Would you," Mason asked, "mind if I looked around?"

Ellen Adair said, "Why, Mr. Mason, I wouldn't think of leaving it *here*."

"I was just asking questions," Mason said.

The lawyer got up, opened a door into a hallway, which disclosed a bathroom and two bedrooms.

"Which one of these is yours?" he asked the young man.

"That one right in front of you there."

Mason went in, sniffed the air a couple of times, walked to the closet and opened the door.

A partially emptied quart bottle of whiskey was on the floor with an ice container and two glasses which still contained ice cubes.

There was lipstick on one of the glasses.

Mason said, "You weren't studying, Wight; you were having a little social gathering. When your mother rang the bell the first time, you had your girl friend get sufficiently presentable so she could leave via the back door. After you let us in the front door, she took your car and drove off."

Wight Baird said, "Suppose you try minding your own business for a change, Mr. Lawyer."

"This *is* my business," Mason said. "I'm trying to get a line on a rather complicated situation."

"All right," Wight said, "so I've been a normal human being. Any law against that?"

"No law against that," Mason said, "but I don't like people who lie to me, and when you, with liquor on your breath, told me this story about having your nose buried in books all day and then I heard someone drive off in your car, I thought perhaps I'd like to check into your story a little bit."

"All right, you've checked it. Now what are you going to do about it?"

"Nothing," Mason said. "I was just testing your truthfulness."

"Wight is a good boy," Ellen Adair said, "but the way boys are tempted these days you just can't blame them for anything. I swear I don't know what girls are thinking of."

Mason turned to Wight. "Do you," he asked, "have the address of Agnes Burlington?"

"I think she left it somewhere. I never paid any attention to it," Wight said.

Mason suddenly whirled and grabbed Wight by the shoulders. "All right," he said, "what did she want? Cut out this lying."

Wight broke loose, said, "Keep your hands off me. I'm not lying."

Mason said, "You're lying and you can get yourself, as well as others, in a lot of trouble. Now what did she want?"

"All right," Wight said in a surly manner; "she wanted money."

"How much money?"

"She wanted ten per cent of whatever I acquired from that Cloverville estate."

"Did you make a deal with her?"

"Well, I . . ."

"*Did* you make a deal with her?" Mason asked.

"All right," Wight said; "I made a deal with her."

"Was there anything in writing?"

"No; she said it would be better not to put it in writing but that if I tried to double-cross her I'd really be sorry."

Mason said, "It would be a big relief if someone somewhere would tell me the truth."

"Well, you move in pretty fast," Wight said.

"I have to move in pretty fast with this family," Mason told him. "Now, have you ever been to Agnes Burlington's place?"

"No."

"You don't know where she lives?"

"Just the address she left—that's all."

"Have you ever had any social dealing with her?"

"What do you mean, social . . . My God, man, the dame was old enough to be my mother. I like them young and snappy and . . . Shucks, no; it was just a business proposition."

"How many times did you see her?"

"Only once in the last month. She came here and . . ."

"And why didn't you tell your mother?"

"She told me not to. She said that Mom was something of a square and old-fashioned and that if she and Mom made any business arrangement the lawyers might find out about it and it would be bad—that, after all, Mom wasn't going to inherit any money. I was the one who was going to get it and . . ."

"Did she tell you how much?"

"A couple of million bucks."

"And you agreed to give her ten per cent?"

"That's right, provided . . ."

"Provided what?"

"Provided she came through with the testimony that would enable me to get it."

Mason said, "In trying to work a deal of that sort, you probably did more to kick your case out of the window than anything that could have happened. Now, then, what about the paper?"

"What paper?"

"She had some kind of a paper, some kind of an agreement," Mason said.

"No, she didn't. I told you that she said it would be better if we didn't have any agreement and . . ."

Mason said, "She had to have something signed by you. She had to have it for her own protection. Now quit lying."

"Well," Wight said, looking at his feet, "she *did* have me give her a memo. She said no agreement or anything —just a memo that would bind the deal."

"And you signed this memo?"

"Yes."

"Was there any copy?"

"No, she said a copy would be dangerous, that there'd be just the one original so that I couldn't go back on the deal, and she'd keep it in a place where it could never be found."

Mason said wearily, "You've done a lot of talking tonight, Wight, and in a short time you've told me more lies than . . ."

"Well, what do you expect—that I'm going to come blurting out with the truth about an arrangement that I'd sworn to keep confidential?"

Mason turned to Della Street. "I guess we can go home now."

"What about me?" Ellen asked.

"You," Mason said, "are to take a taxi back home. You are not to do anything in any way which would result in trying to destroy or tamper with evidence. And, above all, you are not to try and change the tires on your car, try to buy new tires, try to swap the tires around from wheel to wheel, or do anything else. Now do you understand that?"

"But if I sit tight that way, then I'd have to admit that—"

"You admit nothing," Mason said. "From the time you are picked up by the police, you state that you have nothing to say, that you will make no statement unless I am present. And, when I am present, I will tell you to say nothing. Now is that understood?"

"I think that puts me in a bad light with the public."

"Sure it does," Mason said, "but it's better to be in a bad light with the public than to—"

"What is this, Mom?" Wight interrupted. "Don't let that man bully you. If you want to tell your story, go ahead and tell it."

"No, no, Wight; you don't understand," Ellen said.

"Was your girl friend going to come back later with your car?" Mason asked Wight.

"Yes," he said, "if you want to be so damn nosy, she was coming back."

"All right," Mason said, "if you want to do something constructive for a change, you can call your mother a taxicab."

Mason nodded to Della and they walked out of the front door of the house.

Chapter Fourteen

IT WAS shortly before noon when Lieutenant Tragg, all smiles, entered Perry Mason's private office, immediately on the heels of Gertie's frenzied ringing of the telephone.

"Hello, Perry. Hello, Della," Lieutenant Tragg said. "Nice morning this morning. How are you folks feeling?"

"Fine," Mason said. "Is there any reason you can't let Gertie announce you? Must you always come busting into my private office, Lieutenant?"

"Always," Lieutenant Tragg said. "The taxpayers take a dim view of a police officer waiting in a lawyer's outer office while the lawyer composes his thoughts or perhaps gets rid of a client out of the side door—so we just come busting on in, as you call it."

Tragg's grin was friendly and affable.

"Well," Mason said, "I don't have any clients to be spirited out of the side door."

"That's right, you don't," Lieutenant Tragg said.

"We're going to pick up your client, Ellen Adair, and I'm afraid, Perry, we're going to have to charge her with murder.

"Now she'll want to have her lawyer present, and I thought it might be nice if you just came along with me . . . make it all cozy like a little family party . . . and it might save us time."

"Where're you going to pick her up?" Mason asked.

"At the department store," Tragg said. "That's where she works. We hate to humiliate her, but, after all, Perry, you know the law is the law."

"I hope you have evidence," Mason said.

"Evidence?" Tragg said. "Why, of course, we have evidence. We wouldn't pick her up without evidence—you know that, Perry—particularly a woman with a responsible position of this sort."

Mason said to Della Street, "You run this store while I'm gone, Della. I might just as well accommodate the lieutenant."

"Well, that's mighty nice of you, Perry," Lieutenant Tragg said. "It's always so inconvenient to have to pick up someone, then have to call a busy lawyer and have him say he can't get there for an hour or an hour and a half or two hours or whatever time limit he fixes so that his client can have an opportunity to think up a good story."

"This time," Mason said, "I'm going to be frank with you, Lieutenant."

"Please do," Tragg said.

"I'm going to advise Ellen Adair to say absolutely nothing. She'll tell her story for the first time on the witness stand, if she is prosecuted."

"Tut, tut, tut," Lieutenant Tragg said; "now that's not a smart thing to do, Perry."

"It may not be smart, but I think it's fair to handle it that way."

"Well, of course, you do what you see fit," Tragg said, "but we're going to ask questions, and some of them she'd better have the answers for."

"She may have the answers, but that's no sign she's going to give them," Mason said. "I'm taking the sole responsibility of telling her not to answer questions."

"Well, it's your funeral," Tragg said. Then he added with a chuckle, "Or is it?"

"Let's hope it's no one's funeral," Mason said. "Let's go."

Tragg said, "I have a squad car downstairs. We'll be taking your client right to Headquarters. You'd like to ride with us?"

"I'll ride with you," Mason said.

The lawyer looked significantly at Della Street and nodded.

"Oh, that's all right," Tragg said, beaming; "go right ahead, Della, and pick up the telephone, call French, Coleman and Swazey, and tell her that we're on our way out there. After all, Perry Mason, as an attorney, has to give some service to his clients. We'll give her that much preparation.

"Come on, Perry."

The two men left the office building. Tragg, in a rare good humor, seated himself in the front seat beside the driver, put Mason in the back seat, and said, "We'll put your client in there, too, when we pick her up, Perry.

We won't try to do any talking until we get to Headquarters."

Tragg turned to the driver. "French, Coleman and Swazey," he said; "the executive offices."

The police car threaded its way through the traffic with skillful handling, then, after a short run, parked in front of a fireplug at the big department store.

"Just wait here," Lieutenant Tragg instructed the driver. "Want to come along, Mason?"

"Certainly," Mason said; "that's why I'm here."

"It is for a fact," Tragg said.

They went to the executive offices.

Tragg marched into the buyer's office, pushed his way past a startled secretary, entered the private office, and said to Ellen Adair, "I guess you know why we're here, Miss Adair."

Mason said, "Ellen, you are going to be arrested for murder. I instruct you as your attorney to say nothing, to answer no questions."

"Well, now, just a minute, just a minute," Lieutenant Tragg said; "there's a formality first. You don't realize how our activities are all being subjected to formula these days.

"Now, Miss Adair, it's my unpleasant duty to tell you that I am arresting you on suspicion of murder—the murder of Agnes Burlington. I want to warn you that you don't have to answer any questions, that you don't have to make any statements, that if you do make any statements they may be used against you. I want you to know that you are entitled to counsel at all times, and, for your information, Mr. Perry Mason, who is your attorney, was picked up by us and was advised that we were going to put you under arrest. He will be with you whenever you are interrogated.

"Now, then, I'm going to have to ask you to come to Headquarters and to advise you that you are under arrest."

Ellen said, "I told you . . ."

"Hold it," Mason interrupted, "hold it, Ellen. We're not saying anything."

"But I told him . . ."

"If you've already told him, he'll remember what you said," Mason warned, "but right now he'd like to get you to say something else."

"Is there any reason why I can't assert my innocence?" she flared.

"Every reason in the world," Mason said. "He'll get you talking on the little things, and the next thing you know you'll be talking on the big things."

"What big things, Counselor?" Tragg asked.

Mason grinned and said, "Some of the big things you've been uncovering."

"Well, now, of course I don't know what you mean by a big thing," Tragg said, "but, for instance, we can prove that Ellen Adair's car was in the driveway there at the Burlington duplex after the ground had become soft: a detective's delight, Mason—it really is. I was very much surprised. We don't ordinarily find anything that perfect."

"Congratulations," Mason said.

"Thank you, thank you very much, Perry. You see, she drove the car in and found the ground was soft and decided to back out, and she's a good driver. Many drivers would have warped the front wheels a little bit, and that would have made them shovel the mud. You know how it is when the front wheels get out of line with the car in soft soil or sand."

Mason nodded.

"But this woman," Tragg said, "went out without turning the steering wheel. She just went in, found the ground was soft, and backed out, slowly and easily, without spinning the rear wheels; and the front wheels were just enough on a slant so that we got perfect impressions of the front wheels as well as the tires on the hind wheels. Of course, after a while the front wheels got into the groove and obliterated the tracks of the hind wheels, but we got enough to make a perfect moulage. And all four wheels left perfect tracks. The ground was just the right consistency."

"Indeed," Mason said; "I thought when I looked at the ground that it was a little too soft and mushy to leave good impressions."

"Well, that, of course, was later," Lieutenant Tragg said. "We figure that the Adair car was parked in the driveway—or perhaps I should say driven into the driveway—and then backed out at just about the time of death."

"When do you place the time of death?" Mason asked.

"That's very tricky," Lieutenant Tragg said, "and you'll probably ask a lot of questions on cross-examination of the autopsy surgeons. But the best they can do with it is about twenty-four to thirty hours before the body was discovered—rigor mortis had already appeared and left and there was, of course, well-settled postmortem lividity. If we knew when she had ingested the last meal it would help a lot, but evidently it was stuff she had cooked up herself there in the duplex and then she had washed the dishes, and so all we can tell is she was killed within about two hours of the time she ingested the food, but we don't know exactly when that was."

"The nature of the food tell you anything?" Mason asked.

"Well, well, well," Tragg said, "this is the complete reversal of the usual order. In place of asking questions of a suspect, the suspect and her attorney are now asking questions of the peace officers. In view of the Supreme Court decisions, Mason, you'd better warn me that anything I say may be used against me."

"Well," Mason said, "if you're interested in apprehending the real murderer, you should be willing to discuss the facts that have been uncovered to date."

"Exactly," Tragg said; "and if you're interested in the administration of justice and in uncovering what you are pleased to describe as the real murderer, perhaps you'd answer a few questions yourself.

"Now, for instance, there's this question of the package at the post office: an envelope mailed to Ellen Adair at General Delivery.

"Ah-hah, I see that jolts you a little, Miss Adair. You didn't think the police were that thorough, did you?"

"A letter?" Mason asked.

"Well," Tragg said, "we think it's more in the nature of a notebook. In fact, it's about the size of a diary, Mason.

"Now, of course, we haven't opened it yet, because,

while we have a search warrant and all of that, there are formalities to be gone through with first when an article has been consigned to the United States mails. You know, the government is a little touchy about the mail service, but we've seen the exterior of the package and it was dropped in a mailbox, addressed to Ellen Adair at General Delivery, and the handwriting of the address on the envelope is that of Miss Adair.

"Now we'll have that envelope opened within an hour or so, and that could bring about quite a change in the situation, particularly if the contents should be a diary kept by Agnes Burlington.

"Intimate acquaintances of Agnes Burlington insist that there was a diary which was kept in a top right-hand drawer of a dresser. We weren't able to uncover a single sign of a diary when we went through the place after the murder, and if it should appear that the package at the post office, addressed by Miss Adair to herself, contains this missing diary—well, you can see what the situation would be, Mason.

"Would you care to make any statement about that package at the post office, Miss Adair?"

"She would not," Mason interposed firmly.

"She can at least say whether it's something she mailed to herself and when she put it in the post office," Tragg said, "because we have the envelope with the handwritten address and all we'd like to know is why she mailed it to herself at General Delivery. Within an hour we'll know the contents of the envelope."

Ellen Adair gave Mason a look which was sick with apprehension.

Mason said, "Miss Adair is making no statement whatever."

"That looks a little bad from the standpoint of public relations, doesn't it?" Lieutenant Tragg asked.

"We're not trying this case in a court of public relations," Mason said. "We're trying it in a court of justice, and I'm not going to let it be tried in the newspapers."

"Well, we seem to be getting nowhere fast," Lieutenant Tragg said.

Mason said, "Let's put the cards on the table, Lieutenant. There are certain reasons why Miss Adair cannot answer questions. There are certain things in connection with her background which have to be kept undisclosed. If she once starts answering questions, she has to disclose matters which are personal and private. Therefore, she is not answering any questions, and that means she is not going to say one word."

"Well, I can appreciate your position," Tragg said. "It's putting the job right on our shoulders of developing the whole case, but I guess that's the way you want it. But these private matters you are talking about certainly can't relate to a potential will contest which is going to come up in the little town of Cloverville, Perry."

"Why not?" Mason asked.

"Why," Tragg said, "that information is in the hands of the police and, I'm afraid, Perry, in the hands of the press. Of course, I don't want to say anything which would reflect in any way upon your client's character, but, after all, evidence is evidence and there's a witness, a Maxine Edfield, whom I think you know, who has given the police some very valuable information relating to motivation and the possibility that Miss Adair here is going to claim that she had a son by Harmon Haslett, who recently left a two-million-dollar estate. Those are all things that enter into the case by way of motivation, and I am wondering if perhaps, since those matters are now going to be public property, Miss Adair would care to comment on them."

"Miss Adair would not care to comment on anything," Mason said.

"Perhaps as her attorney *you* would care to make some comment?"

"As her attorney I would not care to make any comment."

Tragg shrugged his shoulders. "Well, we seem to have run up against a wall of silence. Of course, you both understand that we are interested in doing justice. We don't want to subject any person to a lot of publicity and a lot of annoyance unless there's some reason for it.

"Now, if Miss Adair could clear up these matters which are bothering the police by simply telling the truth, we'd be only too glad to listen to her explanation, carefully investigate any facts she may give, and wipe the slate clean in the event our investigation warrants."

"You know and I know," Mason said, "that you wouldn't have gone this far unless you had decided to prosecute her for the murder of Agnes Burlington. You know that all this high-sounding malarkey about the administration of justice is simply bait to get the defendant to talk, and it's because of that kind of bait and that kind of malarkey that the courts have established rules that the police have to follow in connection with interrogating a suspect."

Tragg grinned. "Well, Mason," he said, "there's no harm in trying, and, as far as you're concerned, Miss Adair, I'm afraid you're going to have to come along with us.

"I may say one thing to you, Mr. Mason, and that is that this dodge of putting incriminating evidence in a letter and sending it by post to a party at General Delivery is an ingenious device which smacks a little bit of legal counsel.

"Of course, I'm not making any accusation, but it has been done before, and it may interest you to know that as a part of police procedure now whenever a person is represented by counsel in a matter of this sort we make it a rule just as a part of general procedure to go to the post office and see if there's any package addressed to that person at General Delivery. If there is, we take steps to get a search warrant from the state courts and an order from the United States postal authorities, in order to open the package and see what's in it.

"I hope for your sake and the sake of your client that when we open that package addressed to Ellen Adair at General Delivery we don't find a diary kept by Agnes Burlington—but I'm just a little afraid, judging from the evidence that we have at hand, that that's what we're going to find.

"And now, Miss Adair, if you will kindly accompany me to Headquarters, we'll try to make the formalities of booking as painless as possible—that is, of course, unless you want to change your mind and explain your actions to me. If there's any logical explanation, we're willing to listen."

"There's no explanation," Mason said, "logical or otherwise. We are standing on our rights to remain silent.

"I want five minutes to confer with my client, Lieutenant. Would you mind waiting in the outer office? Then I'll surrender her and you can take her to Headquarters."

"After they're once arrested you're supposed to have your conferences with them in a conference room at the detention ward," Tragg said.

"That's after they're booked," Mason told him. "Of course, if you want to adopt the position that you're refusing to let me confer with my client, then I . . ."

"No, no, not at all," Tragg said; "we're not walking into any trap today—not if we can help it. You want five minutes?"

"Five minutes."

"I'll give you five minutes," Tragg said, and, bowing sardonically, stepped out into the other office.

Mason turned to Ellen Adair. "Is Agnes Burlington's diary in that envelope?"

"Yes."

"Where did you get it?"

"Out of the top bureau drawer."

"All right," Mason said; "now, you went there earlier. You found her dead. You made a search. You picked up the diary."

"Yes."

"Was there a gun anywhere there?"

"No."

"Do you own a gun?"

"Why, yes."

"What kind of a gun?"

"A thirty-eight-caliber Colt."

"Where is it now?"

"Heavens, I don't know. Somewhere in my apartment, I guess. I . . . no, I remember now. I loaned it to Wight. He wanted to do some target practicing. He was taking a girl out on a picnic and—well, he's an awfully good shot and I guess he wanted to show off a little bit."

"What did he do with the gun? Did he give it back?"

"No, he still has it, unless . . . oh, my God!"

"What now?" Mason asked.

"I remember now. He told me that he was going to put it in the glove compartment of my car when he got done with it."

"Do you know if he did it?"

"No, but I presume he did."

"Then when the police impounded your car they could have found a thirty-eight-caliber revolver in it?"

"I guess they could have."

Mason said, "If it should turn out that that revolver is the fatal weapon, there's nothing anybody can do that will save you. A jury is going to bring in a verdict of first-degree murder."

"I . . . I guess you think I've been rather stupid, don't you, Mr. Mason?"

"That," Mason said, "is a very good appraisal of the situation. You've tried to be smart, and all you've done is outsmarted yourself."

The lawyer stepped to the door of the outer office.

"Only three and a half minutes," Tragg said cheerfully.

"That's good," Mason told him grimly. "Keep the change. You can have what's left."

Chapter Fifteen

MASON sat in his office, shirt open at the neck, the remnants of a cup of coffee in front of him.

Paul Drake sat in the client's overstuffed chair, making notes. Della Street opened a sealed package, put a new charge of coffee in the percolator.

Mason, dog-tired, said, "I'm stuck with this woman, Paul. I walked into the case blind and I can't get out.

"Now, then, I can't tell you all that the police have on her because probably I don't know, but the big thing I have to find out is whether the police have located the fatal weapon."

"Your client have a gun?" Drake asked.

"That," Mason said, "is only part of the question. She has a thirty-eight-caliber Colt revolver which was bought in an open market at a reputable gun store, and the store's firearm record will show she has that gun."

"Where is it?" Drake asked.

"Probably in the hands of the police," Mason said.

"Now, then, Paul, the thing I absolutely have to find out is whether that gun fired the fatal bullet."

"And if it did?" Drake asked.

"If it did," Mason said, "the only thing I can do is to try to cop a plea. There isn't one chance in ten thousand that a jury would acquit Ellen Adair."

"And if it isn't the fatal gun?"

"If it isn't the fatal gun," Mason said, "we've got to be able to prove that it isn't the fatal gun.

"The fact that she had a gun and the fact that the gun is presumably the same type of gun which was used in the murder—by that I mean it wasn't an automatic and didn't eject a cartridge—and all of the other things combined are going to make quite a case of circumstantial evidence."

"But it'll still be circumstantial evidence," Drake said.

"Circumstantial evidence," Mason told him, "is, as a matter of fact, about the strongest evidence we have. The big trouble with circumstantial evidence lies in its interpretation."

Drake said, "I understand from a confidential source that the police are going to be able to show that Ellen Adair's automobile was parked in Agnes Burlington's driveway and that Ellen Adair was inside the house long before the police were notified.

"The assumption of the prosecution is going to be that there was some evidence she wanted suppressed or changed in some way and that Ellen Adair came and got you and you went with her to the scene of the crime, fixed things the way you wanted them to be found by the police, and then notified the police."

"They'll adopt that attitude," Mason said. "It's an unjust attitude and an uncharitable attitude as far as an attorney-at-law is concerned, but, nevertheless, there's enough evidence to support it, so they'll adopt it."

"Can they prove that her car was there and that she was in the place?" Drake asked. "If they can, it looks pretty tough, unless you can do some mighty fast talking by way of explanation."

Mason said, "It's just another piece of circumstantial evidence, and there are lots of bits of evidence. For instance, Paul, I think the circumstantial evidence will show that Agnes Burlington met her death within about two hours after she had eaten a meal. I want to know what that meal consisted of and what time it was eaten."

"How are you going to prove that?"

"There's a supermarket nearby. I think probably she ran in there from time to time for provisions. See what you can find out there."

"Think they'll remember her at the supermarket?" Drake asked.

"It's a chance worth taking," Mason said. "I have an idea that we're dealing with a woman living alone who would go into the supermarket, pick up a few odds and ends, perhaps one of these complete frozen dinners, take it home, put it in the oven until it was ready to serve, then eat—that is, when she was eating by herself.

"Now, then, the police have been a little bit reluctant to give out information about the contents of the stomach. I think perhaps there's a clue in their reluctance.

"If she had eaten a steak dinner with French fried potatoes, a salad and perhaps a dish of vegetables, it would indicate that she had been out with some man, in which event the man would have escorted her back to her duplex house."

"But you don't know whether it was a dinner she ate as her last meal or a lunch or a breakfast."

"I know that the lights had been left on," Mason said, "and that leads me to believe that the crime took place sometime in the evening; and if that was within two hours of the time the meal was ingested, it probably was the sort of meal she'd get when she didn't want to be bothered with a lot of cooking and a lot of dishes.

"If, on the other hand, the meal was one that would have cost from three to six dollars in a restaurant, I have an idea she was out with a man."

"That's good reasoning," Drake said.

"Therefore," Mason told him, "a lot depends on the nature of the meal. Circumstantial evidence can be tricky sometimes, but it never gives you a complete double cross the way some people will, and two million dollars is quite a temptation to anyone."

Drake nodded. "Anything else?"

Mason looked at his watch. "Nothing, except to get some sleep, Paul. Try and find out what you can."

Drake said, "I know one thing: they're having trouble finding the fatal bullet."

Mason's eyes widened. "But they *have* to find it, Paul."

"That's what Lieutenant Tragg has told his officers, but they've sifted everything in the house, and I understand, off the record, they are a little chagrined because they can't find the fatal bullet."

Mason said, "It's in there someplace. They'll dig it up.

I certainly would like to know if it matches with any gun they've uncovered in the case."

"I think I've got a pipeline in to the police. I may not be able to get you a lot of detailed information, but I think I can let you know if they have the fatal bullet and whether it matches the gun."

"See what you can do," Mason said.

Drake unwound his tall figure from his chair, said, "I'll be in touch, Perry," and went out.

Della Street regarded the lawyer with troubled eyes. "Can you afford to put Ellen Adair on the witness stand?" she asked.

"No," Mason said, "not the way things are looking now. The district attorney would tear her to pieces on cross-examination. She's put herself in an impossible position and, so far, the circumstantial evidence is all against her."

"What can you do if you can't put her on the stand?"

Mason said, "There's one nice thing about circumstantial evidence; it's a two-edged sword. It cuts both ways, and it always tells the truth. The trouble with circumstantial evidence is that sometimes we make an incorrect interpretation because we don't have all the evidence.

"However, Della, I'm just nursing one theory which I'm hoping against hope will pan out."

"Want to talk?" she asked.

Mason got up from behind his desk, started pacing the floor. "I want to talk," he said. "You're a jury. I'm a lawyer representing the defense."

"All right," she said; "go ahead."

Mason said, "The district attorney tells you that he has unmistakable circumstantial evidence that the defendant came to the home of Agnes Burlington, parked her car in the driveway, and went in to see the woman who was murdered.

"The prosecution has introduced moulage exhibits, and there seems to be no question that the automobile belonging to the defendant was actually driven into the driveway of the Burlington house.

"Now, I'll ask you the question: *when* was it driven?

"At first blush you may think we can't answer that question—that is, that we can't answer it with reference to the time of death—but I think we can.

"The evidence shows that Agnes Burlington was in the habit of watering her lawn in the evening. She had an underground system, and it was her habit to turn this on so that just a mere trickle of water was coming out from the various outlets. She would then leave this water on until she went to bed, when she would turn it off."

"Can I ask a question?" Della Street said.

"Jurors can always ask questions," Mason said, smiling. "What is your question, Miss Juror?"

"How do we know that it was her custom to turn on the water in the evening and turn it off when she went to bed?"

"We don't as yet," Mason said, "but I think the evidence indicates that that's what happened this night, and I think—in fact, I hope—we can show that it was her custom."

"Go ahead," Della Street said

"Now, then," Mason said, "the particular night in question, the one we're interested in, Agnes Burlington didn't turn off the water; she didn't turn off the electric lights."

"Why?"

"The answer has to be because she was alive when she turned on the water, she was alive when she turned on the lights; but when the time came when she would normally turn off the water and normally turn off the lights she was dead. Moreover, weather records show there was a violent thundershower on the evening of the fourth. This is an unusual event for this climate; but there was the usual violent wind, the usual brief, drenching rain.

"If Agnes Burlington had been alive after that drenching rain, she would have turned off the water on the lawn. And the noise of the thunder could have prevented any neighbors from hearing the shot.

"Therefore, the water ran all night on the lawn, all the next morning. The lights were on all that night, all the next morning. Then Ellen Adair drove up to see Agnes Burlington.

"We can't *prove* the exact time that Ellen Adair parked her car, but we do know that it must have been many hours after Agnes Burlington's death, because the water, turned on so that it would trickle through the watering system onto the lawn, had soaked the lawn and then had drained down into the driveway so that it had left the driveway so muddy that the soil had retained the prints of the tires on the defendant's car when she had driven in.

"In other words, ladies and gentlemen of the jury, the evidence conclusively shows that Ellen Adair must have driven her car into that driveway twelve to fifteen hours *after* Agnes Burlington had met her death."

Mason paused. "How am I doing?" he asked.

"Very well," Della said. "But won't Ellen tell you what time she drove in there and left those tracks?"

"Sure she will. She has. She says it was just an hour or two before she came here to the office to tell me about Agnes Burlington.

"I think that's another lie. She's either trying to protect her son or is distorting the evidence.

"I have to prepare this case for a jury without relying on any outside help. I have to rely on the evidence."

"You're doing fine," Della Street said. "My verdict is *not guilty!*"

Mason grinned. "You're a little too easily persuaded by defense's arguments, Della. But, so far, that's our only hope to cling to—that and the hope that the fatal bullet wasn't fired from the revolver that the police found in the glove compartment of Ellen Adair's car."

"Suppose it turns out that the fatal bullet was fired from that gun?"

"Then," Mason said, "we've got to find some dramatic development which is going to indicate innocence; otherwise we're licked."

"What about Wight Baird?" Della Street asked. "Couldn't he have fired the fatal bullet?"

"Sure he could," Mason said, "and for all we know he did. There's a modern young man who wants to go through life the easy way. I don't know how much the Bairds left him, but if it wasn't a substantial amount he could have pretty well gone through it. And if it was a substantial amount he could have decided that a couple of million more might be very acceptable."

"But, then, why would he kill Agnes Burlington, whose testimony would establish his claim to the two million?"

"How do we know her testimony would have established his claim?" Mason asked. "We have the word of Ellen Adair for it, but how many times has Ellen Adair lied to us?"

Della Street nodded. "You have a point there," she said.

"Well," Mason said, "the preliminary examination starts tomorrow, and by that time we'll find out a lot more about the case."

"You won't try to get the case dismissed?" Della Street asked.

"Not with all this evidence piled up against our client," Mason said. "Not unless we can get some sort of a break."

"Well, we can always hope," Della Street said.

"The whole thing turns on that fatal bullet," Mason said, "whether it was fired from Ellen Adair's gun or whether it wasn't."

"What does Wight say about the gun?"

"What you'd expect him to say," Mason said. "He borrowed the gun for target practice a week or ten days earlier. He fired the gun several times, then put it back in the glove compartment of Ellen Adair's car, where he had told Ellen he'd leave it. Natural enough in one way when you consider his youth, his diversification of interests, girl friends, studies, hot-rod automobiles, and liquor."

Della said, "I shudder to think of what that young man would do with two million dollars in cash."

Mason regarded her thoughtfully. "Look at it from his standpoint," he said.

"What do you mean?"

"Figure out what he'd do *without* two million dollars in cash."

Chapter Sixteen

JUDGE DEAN ELWELL took his position on the bench, glanced at his court calendar, said, "The case of the People of the State of California versus Ellen Calvert, also known as Ellen Adair, defendant."

"Ready for the defendant," Perry Mason said.

Stanley Cleveland Dillon, the chief trial deputy of the district attorney's office, stood up with impressive dignity.

"We are ready for the people," he said. "And the people respectfully wish to point out that this is a preliminary hearing solely for the purpose of determining whether a crime has been committed and whether there are reasonable grounds to determine that the defendant has committed that crime."

Judge Elwell said with some acerbity, "The Court understands the rule of law, Mr. Dillon."

"I know the Court does," Dillon said. "But I wanted to point out the position that the prosecution will take when it comes to combating the harassing, delaying tactics which are so much a part of the defense in some of these cases."

"We won't go into any personalities," Judge Elwell ruled. "Call your first witness."

Stanley Dillon, who prided himself upon having sent more defendants to their deaths than any other trial deputy in the State of California, was visibly annoyed at Judge Elwell's treatment.

Of late, there had been some criticism that Dillon regarded defendants in criminal cases as so much game to be stalked. Then an irate defense attorney had remarked that if it had been legal Dillon would have disinterred the bodies, mounted the heads of the various defendants whom he had sent to the gas chamber, and had them arranged as trophies in his study.

Criticism of this sort bothered Dillon and caused him to explain that he was only doing his duty as a public servant. He claimed that he took no personal satisfaction whatever in securing verdicts of death in the criminal cases he had prosecuted. He was very conscious of public relations.

Now he was well aware of the crowded courtroom.

Not only had the case attracted much public attention because of newspaper publicity and the issues involved, but the two half brothers of Harmon Haslett, Bruce and Norman Jasper, were present in court, as were "Slick" Garland, the troubleshooter, and Jarmen Dayton, the detective.

Ellen Adair sat beside Mason, still maintaining that air

of queenly dignity, divorcing herself as a person from the proceedings in which she was the accused.

"I am, if the Court pleases, going to make this as brief as possible," Dillon said. "I will call Lieutenant Tragg as my first witness."

Lieutenant Tragg came forward, took the oath, seated himself comfortably in the witness stand, and gave his name, address and occupation to the clerk.

"I am going to ask you, Lieutenant, very briefly to tell the Court what you found when you were called to a duplex dwelling at 1635 Manlay Avenue on the fifth of the month. I will ask you to describe briefly what you found."

"Very well," Lieutenant Tragg said. "We found a house with a front door which was closed and locked with a spring lock. The back door, however, was unlocked and partially open. We found a typical duplex bungalow, and in the bedroom of the bungalow, where all windows were closed and locked, we found the body of the occupant of the duplex."

"Her name, please."

"Agnes Burlington."

"What was the condition of the body, Lieutenant?"

"It was clothed in a garter girdle, a bra, stockings and shoes."

"How was the body lying?"

"Somewhat on its left side, generally in a face-down position."

"What was the condition of the body medically?"

"The medical examiner can tell you more about that," Lieutenant Tragg said. "But, generally, rigor mortis appeared to have formed and disappeared. There was post-mortem lividity."

"What did the postmortem lividity indicate?"

"That the body had not been moved after death."

"You took photographs?"

"We took many photographs, showing the position of the body and the surroundings."

"Now, when you moved the body, what did you find?"

Lieutenant Tragg knew that he was dropping a bomb-shell in the lap of the defense. He couldn't resist glancing at Perry Mason to see how the defense lawyer would take the information.

"We found a thirty-two-caliber Smith and Wesson re-volver under the body."

Mason jerked bolt upright in his chair. "May I ask the court reporter to read that last answer?" Mason asked.

"Very well," Judge Elwell ruled.

The court reporter read the answer: "We found a thirty-two-caliber Smith and Wesson revolver under the body."

"Was that revolver the fatal weapon?" Dillon asked.

"I object, if the Court pleases," Mason said. "This calls for a conclusion of the witness, and no proper foundation has been laid for his examination as a ballistics expert; nor has there been any evidence that the decedent met her death by means of a gunshot wound. Therefore, the question assumes facts not in evidence."

"Oh, if the Court please," Dillon said, "this is simply an attempt to expedite matters. I suppose that I could ask Lieutenant Tragg as to the cause of death and he could state that it was a bullet wound, but defense counsel would probably object on the ground that I had not qualified him as an autopsy surgeon."

"Go ahead; ask him," Mason invited.

"What was the cause of death?" Dillon asked.

"A gunshot wound."

Dillon said wearily, "At this time I'll withdraw Lieutenant Tragg from the stand temporarily and put on the autopsy surgeon."

"Just a minute," Mason said. "I have a few questions I would like to ask of Lieutenant Tragg on cross-examination before he steps down."

"You'll have an opportunity to cross-examine him when I'm finished," Dillon said irritably.

"But I would like to cross-examine him now as to certain phases of the testimony he has already given. If you are going to ask him to step down from the stand, I think that I have that right," Mason said.

"All right, all right, all right," Dillon said testily. "I have no objection."

Mason said, "You found a gun under the body of the decedent, Lieutenant Tragg?"

"That's right. Yes, sir."

"And that gun was a thirty-two-caliber Smith and Wesson revolver?"

"Yes, sir."

"What about the cylinder?"

"The gun was fully loaded."

"There were no empty cartridges in the cylinder?"

"No."

"Had the gun been discharged recently?"

"According to the best tests we could make, the gun had not been discharged in some time."

"And did you make any attempt to trace the registration of that gun?"

"We did. Yes, sir."

"And who had originally purchased that gun?"

"The decedent, Agnes Burlington, had purchased it some years ago when she was a nurse in San Francisco and was called upon to go home from nursing jobs at various hours of the night."

"She had permission to carry the weapon?"

"She did when she purchased it and for some years thereafter in San Francisco; but she did not have a permit to carry the gun at the time of her death."

"This revolver was a thirty-two-caliber?" Mason asked.

"That's right."

"Is it possible that the decedent could have met her death with a bullet from that gun and that thereafter someone could have removed the empty cartridge case and inserted a full cartridge in the cylinder?"

Lieutenant Tragg shifted his position on the witness stand, then said, "I would say not."

"Why?" Mason asked.

"Well, in the first place, I think she was shot with a thirty-eight-caliber revolver. I think we have the murder weapon. In the second place, I don't think that this thirty-two-caliber Smith and Wesson had been fired at any time within the last five or six weeks."

"You recovered the fatal bullet?" Mason asked casually.

"Now, just a minute—just a minute!" Dillon said. "If the Court pleases, I want to object to this on the ground that it is not proper cross-examination. I haven't as yet gone into the question of the make or the caliber of the gun which inflicted the fatal wound or the whereabouts of the fatal bullet. I have been stopped by Counsel's objections. Therefore, defense Counsel has no right to cross-examine the witness on these points."

"Well, if you want to be technical about it, I presume the Court will have to rule with you," Judge Elwell said. "The objection is sustained."

"Very well," Mason said, "that's all at this time."

Dillon said, "I will call Dr. Leland Clinton as my next witness."

Dr. Clinton—a tall, efficient-appearing individual with an air of icy composure—took the witness stand; gave his name, address and occupation; recited his professional qualifications in response to questions laying the foundation to qualify him as an expert; and was then asked if he had performed the autopsy on the body of Agnes Burlington.

"I did. Yes, sir."

"Now, then, Doctor," Dillon said, "I don't want technical terms; I want to know generally the cause of death."

"The cause of death," Dr. Clinton said, "was a gunshot wound. A bullet entered the back to the right of the median line, penetrated the very top of the right kidney ranging upward, penetrated the heart, and emerged from the left side of the upper chest. I can, of course, give you the course of the bullet anatomically with—"

"Not at this time, Doctor," Dillon said. "I don't care to clutter up the record with a lot of technical terminology unless the defendant should ask for it. The wound inflicted by this bullet, as you have described it, was sufficient to cause death?"

"Yes."

"Within what length of time?"

"Death was practically instantaneous—a matter of perhaps two or three seconds."

"Could the decedent have moved after having sustained this wound?"

"Very briefly perhaps, but I doubt if the decedent could have engaged in many physical activities. From a physical standpoint, death was practically instantaneous."

"Now, then, the course of the bullet was ranging upward."

"That is right."

"So the weapon from which the bullet was fired must have been held at a low angle. If the decedent was standing at the time, the murder weapon must have been pressed close to the body at about the level of the waist or a little lower."

"Yes, sir."

"You may cross-examine," Dillon said.

"Were there any powder burns on the body of the decedent at the wound of entrance?" Mason asked.

"No."

"Then the weapon couldn't have been held close to the body of the decedent."

"I didn't say that it had been."

"Pardon me," Mason said. "I thought you said in response to a question by the prosecutor that if the body had been in a standing position, the weapon must have been held at about the level of the waist."

"That is correct," Dr. Clinton said. "I am assuming, in answering that question, that it relates only to conditions *if* the decedent had been standing."

"But if she had been standing, there would have been powder burns?"

"We would have reasonably expected powder burns —depending somewhat on the distance of the murder weapon from the body of the decedent. The murderer could, for instance, have held the weapon at the level of the floor, and there would have been no powder burns. But ordinarily, if the decedent had been in a standing position, there should have been powder burns—that is, we would have expected to find them."

"Then your assumption is that the decedent was not in a standing position at the time of her death?"

"It is possible, yes."

"And what could have been her position?"

"Once we eliminate the question of a standing position, she could have been in any position. She could have been on all fours, she could have been lying on the floor, or she could have been lying in bed."

"Did you find any evidence of contusions indicating that she had been struck or knocked down?"

"No."

"And the bullet emerged from the upper left chest?"

"That is correct."

"What about the contents of the stomach, Doctor?" Mason asked.

"Now, just a moment!" Dillon said. "Here again Counsel is anticipating the prosecution's case. I would like to put on my case in an orderly manner. I haven't as yet asked this witness anything about the time of death."

"Well, you're going to have to come to it," Judge Elwell said.

"I would like to present the case in an orderly manner
—showing first the fact of death, the cause of death, and
then the time of death."

"I don't think I care to hear the case piecemeal," Judge
Elwell said, "unless there is some particular reason for
putting it on in this manner."

"I can assure the Court that there is a reason," Dillon
said.

"Very well. But that doesn't prevent Counsel from asking this witness any questions he cares to about the *condition* of the body; and I will permit questions concerning
the contents of the stomach."

Dillon said, "If the Court is going to permit those
questions, I may as well go right ahead and show the time
of death."

"Well, Counsel has asked a question and he's entitled
to an answer," Judge Elwell said. "The witness will answer the question."

"The contents of the stomach," Dr. Clinton said,
"showed green peas, scallops, potatoes, and bread."

"In what state of preservation?" Mason asked. "In other
words, how far had digestion progressed?"

"Death had taken place within approximately thirty
minutes of the time the meal had been ingested."

Judge Elwell said, "There was no objection to that
question, Mr. Mason; but I think you are probably tech-
nically restricted in your cross-examination as to matters
which were brought out on direct examination and the

physical condition of the body. I understand the prosecutor wants to proceed with evidence showing the time of death."

"Very well," Mason said. "Under those circumstances, I have no further cross-examination at this time."

"All right," Stanley Dillon said, "I may as well go into the time of death. How long had the decedent been dead before your examination?"

"I would say between twenty-four and thirty-six hours."

"Could you make it any closer than that?"

"Not from a standpoint of accurate evidence, no. I would be somewhat inclined to fix the time of death as approximately twenty-four hours before the body was discovered."

"And the body was discovered at about eight-twenty on the evening of the fifth?"

"As to that, I know only by hearsay. I know that I performed my autopsy at seven o'clock on the morning of the sixth; and I would generally fix the time of death as from twenty-four to thirty-six hours previous to my examination."

"Can you tell whether the body had been moved after death?"

"In my opinion, the body had not been moved after death unless it had been moved almost immediately after the fatal shot had been fired."

"What causes you to have that opinion, Doctor?"

"Because of postmortem lividity. After death, the blood becomes discolored and settles in the lower part of the body. In other words, after the heart ceases to function, the forces of gravitation take over and the blood has a tendency to settle in the body and become discolored. There was a well-defined postmortem lividity here, indicating that the body had not been moved—unless it was moved very shortly after the fatal wound had been inflicted."

"I think that's all at this time," Dillon said.

"Did you form any opinion as to the caliber of the fatal bullet?" Mason asked.

"These things are very, very tricky," Dr. Clinton said. "My personal opinion is that the bullet was a thirty-eight-caliber bullet; but the skin is elastic during lifetime and it is difficult without examining the fatal bullet itself to be sure as to its caliber."

"And there was no fatal bullet in the body?" Mason asked.

"No. The bullet had emerged from the upper left chest, as I stated in my earlier testimony."

"Thank you, Doctor. That's all."

"Now, then, I'll recall Lieutenant Tragg," Dillon said. Tragg again took the stand.

"When did you arrive at 1635 Manlay Avenue, Lieutenant?"

"At eight forty-seven on the evening of the fifth."

"You made an examination of the premises?"

"I did."

"Did you meet the defendant there at that time?"

"I did."

"Did you discuss with her what she had observed and why she had gone there?"

"Generally, yes."

"And, at that time, your inquiries were simply general. You had not determined upon the defendant as a suspect at that time."

"That is correct."

"Did she tell you anything about her time of arrival?"

"She said that she had come there with Mr. Perry Mason and Miss Della Street, Perry Mason's secretary; that they had found the woman dead and had promptly called police."

"Did she say anything at any time about having been there earlier?"

"No, sir. She gave us to understand this was her first visit to the place in some time."

"Did she say anything to you about having taken a diary or any other personal property from the premises?"

"On the contrary, she said they had left things just as they found them."

"Did you try to develop latent fingerprints?"

"Yes, sir."

"Were you able to develop any?"

"Yes, sir."

"Were you able to identify any of the latent prints you developed?"

"Yes, sir. There were fingerprints of the decedent, of course; there were fingerprints of some individual who has not been identified; and there were fingerprints of a man named Ralph Corning, who is—so to speak—a boy-friend of the decedent and who had been there earlier in the week but who was out of town on the third, fourth and fifth."

"Any other fingerprints?"

"Those of the defendant," the witness said, "and some others that were smudged—but many good fingerprints of the defendant."

"Where did you find them?"

"Generally, we found them on the bureau drawers, on the doorknob, on the woodwork, on the glass panel of the front door."

"Inside or outside?"

"Inside. We also found latent fingerprints of the defendant where she had pressed her hands against the glass of the front window.

"I have here a set of photographs all properly identified by markings upon the backs of the pictures, showing the various localities in which we found the fingerprints in question and some enlargements of the fingerprints themselves."

"Did you at any time, at any place, find a diary which apparently had been kept by the decedent?"

"We did; yes, sir."

"Where did you find that?"

"We found it in the post office at the General Delivery window on the morning of the sixth."

"Did you identify it at that time?"

"No, sir; we simply asked for mail that was addressed to the defendant, Ellen Adair. When we found that there was such mail, we secured a search warrant; then we made arrangements with the federal post office authorities and eventually got an envelope open which contained a diary in the handwriting of the decedent."

"What was the address on that envelope?"

"Ellen Adair, General Delivery."

"Do you know whose handwriting that was in?"

"I cannot qualify as an expert on handwriting," Lieutenant Tragg said, "but I have had some experience. The handwriting generally appears to be that of the defendant. I believe it has been submitted to a handwriting expert who will testify later on."

"You made photographs of the location of the body?"

"We did. Here they are."

"We ask that all these photographs be introduced in evidence," Dillon said, "and that the clerk be instructed to give them appropriate exhibit numbers."

"So ordered," Judge Elwell said.

"Did you find a revolver in the possession of the defendant?"

"There was a thirty-eight-caliber revolver found in the glove compartment of the defendant's automobile."

"Was that revolver loaded?"

"There were five full cartridges and one empty cartridge chamber in the cylinder."

"No exploded cartridge in that one chamber?"

"No, it was empty. The shell case had been removed."

"You personally made tests with that gun?"

"Yes, sir."

"What was your opinion as to when it had been last fired?"

"It had been fired within three days of the time we picked it up."

"How did you determine that?"

"Chemical analysis of the residue of cartridge primer, residue of gas, condition of the barrel, and the smell of exploded smokeless powder."

"I think you may inquire on cross-examination," Dillon said.

Mason said, "There was no bullet found in the body?"

"No, sir."

"And no bullet found in the room?"

"No, sir."

"But the bullet had gone entirely through the body of the decedent?"

Lieutenant Tragg, who had evidently been anticipating this series of questions and was fully prepared for them, smiled affably. "Yes, sir. This was one of those cases of which, unfortunately, there are too many—where there is no recovery of the fatal bullet."

"What do you mean by that?" Mason asked. "What do you mean there are altogether too many such cases?"

Tragg went on glibly with his explanation. "The average cartridge case," he said, "contains powder which, upon ignition, is used as a propellant. The amount of powder is such that in the average weapon with a barrel of three to five inches the explosive energy is almost all expended in forcing a bullet through the body of a human being, so that quite frequently we find cases where the bullet has gone entirely through the body but has been stopped by the elasticity of the skin when it starts to emerge from the inner tissues and the bullet is trapped just beneath the skin of the decedent.

"At other times there is just enough propellant to push the bullet through the outer skin and then the bullet does not leave the immediate proximity but is trapped within the clothing of the decedent. It either falls out unnoticed in the vehicle which takes the decedent to the morgue or it is spilled out someplace else in the course of transit. Perhaps it may fall unnoticed to the floor of the autopsy room."

"You say it can be trapped in the clothes," Mason said.

"Yes, sir."

"However, in this case," Mason said, "the decedent was wearing no clothes which could conceivably have trapped a bullet. Is that right?"

"Generally speaking, that is correct," Tragg said, "but, of course, numerous other things could have happened to the bullet."

"What, for instance?"

"The bullet could have just emerged from the skin of the upper left chest of the decedent, fallen to the floor, and been kicked around by some of the first people who were on the scene."

"Officers?" Mason asked.

Tragg said grimly, "I said the *first* people who were on the scene."

"And where would the bullet have been kicked to?"

"It could have been kicked under a bureau or under the bed or it could have been picked up."

"Why would anyone have picked up a fatal bullet?" Mason asked.

Tragg smiled and said affably, "So that it couldn't be fitted to the fatal gun."

"That, of course, is surmise on your part," Mason said.

"You're asking for surmises," Tragg told him. "There is also the possibility that the bullet could have been in the pool of coagulated blood which was on the floor and which was scraped up in its entirety and disposed of.

The bullet could also have fallen out on the stretcher on which the body was taken to the car that went to the morgue. Then when the body was slid into the wagon the stretcher could have been handled in such a way that the bullet rolled off and fell to the lawn, and since the lawn was soft and muddy the bullet might have been trampled into the ground."

Mason said, "Was any search made for the bullet after it appeared that it was not in the body?"

Tragg smiled. "We tore everything to pieces inside that room. We looked in every bureau drawer, we shook out every article of clothing that was hanging in the closet, we went through every inch of wall space. We even looked in the upholstery and at the drapes."

"You say the drapes. Were they pulled?"

"Yes. The decedent was evidently getting ready to take a bath and was undressing at the time of her death. The drapes were drawn, the windows were closed and locked from the inside."

"What about the ceiling?" Mason said. "If the gun had been held down on the floor and the course of the bullet ranged upward, the bullet might have penetrated the ceiling."

"We searched that thoroughly," Tragg said. "We made a *very* thorough search. We were unable to find the bullet."

"So you can't tell that the gun which you found in the defendant's automobile was the fatal gun?"

"We can't prove it absolutely—the way we could have if we had recovered the fatal bullet," Tragg said; "but we are able to prove it by circumstantial evidence. The vacant space in the cylinder from which a cartridge had been removed, the fact that the gun had recently been fired, the fact that the fatal bullet was evidently a thirty-eight-caliber bullet—all of these are circumstances . . . significant circumstances."

Mason said, "You have heard the testimony of the autopsy surgeon that the decedent could hardly have moved after the bullet entered her body, that death was practically instantaneous."

"Yes, sir."

"Yet there was a gun found underneath the defendant's body."

"Yes, sir."

"The defendant's own gun."

"Yes, sir."

"Have you in your investigations found how that gun came to be in that position?"

"No, sir; it could have been placed there by someone who took it from a bureau drawer and then pushed it under the body after the decedent met her death."

"Or conceivably," Mason said, "the decedent could have been holding it in her hand, pointing it at someone whom she was threatening or someone who had been threatening her, and for the moment had her attention distracted and—"

"And she turned her back," Tragg supplemented with a grin, "on another person who was holding a thirty-eight-caliber revolver in a threatening position."

"Exactly," Mason said.

"I suppose something of that sort is conceivable," Lieutenant Tragg said, "but I would hardly consider it within the realm of possibility."

"In this diary which you recovered," Mason said, "did you find any significant passages?"

"Lots of them."

"Anything dealing with the defendant?"

"Yes, there were two entries in which the decedent stated that she had collected from Ellen Adair and that contributions were becoming exceedingly and progressively difficult."

"That's all," Mason said abruptly. "I have no further cross-examination."

"Call Maxine Edfield to the stand," Dillon said.

"What is the purpose of this witness?" Judge Elwell asked.

"To show motivation, Your Honor."

"Very well, I'll hear this witness," Judge Elwell said, "but as you yourself pointed out, Mr. Prosecutor, this is just a preliminary hearing for the purpose of determining whether there are reasonable grounds for believing that, first, a crime was committed and, second, the defendant was connected with that crime.

"This is not a hearing before a jury where the prosecution is called upon to prove its case beyond all reasonable doubt; and I may state that, as far as this Court is concerned, the evidence of that diary's having been removed and mailed in an envelope addressed to the defendant, coupled with the evidence of the gun in the glove compartment of defendant's car, is sufficient to warrant an order holding the defendant over."

"I think, if the Court pleases, we would like to either introduce evidence or argue the case," Mason said.

"I don't see what there is to argue," Judge Elwell said. "At this time we aren't dealing with the credibility of witnesses. The law is that all the testimony of the prosecution is to be taken at its face value for the purpose of this hearing."

"Am I to be precluded from arguing the case?"

"No, not at all," Judge Elwell said testily. "I am simply trying to tell you that your argument may not do much good, and I am trying to expedite the hearing. If the deputy prosecutor feels that this witness can show motivation, I will be willing to hear at least some testimony directed to this point.

"Certainly the prosecution doesn't intend to disclose its entire case at this point—only enough to have an order binding the defendant over for trial in the Supreme Court. You may go ahead, Mr. Prosecutor. Question this witness. What is her name?"

"Maxine Edfield."

"Very well," Judge Elwell ruled, "go ahead with your examination."

Maxine Edfield seemed bursting with a desire to tell her story and, from the first question asked by the prosecutor, launched into a long dissertation.

"Do you," the prosecutor asked, "know Ellen Adair, the defendant, and, if so, how long have you known her?"

"I know the defendant," Maxine said. "She is now going by the name of Ellen Adair. When I knew her she was Ellen Calvert, and that is her real name. At that time I was very friendly with her, and she was keeping company with a man by the name of Harmon Haslett, who was the son of Ezekiel Haslett, who was the founder and owner of the Cloverville Spring and Suspension Company.

"At that time she was being intimate with young Haslett, and when he began to cool off she decided to pretend to be pregnant and—"

"Now, just a minute, just a minute!" Judge Elwell interrupted. "I think we'd better go ahead by question and answer and give opposing counsel a chance to object."

"Let her go, as far as we're concerned," Perry Mason said. "I think I can clarify the situation with a few questions on cross-examination, but, as far as her story is concerned, she has told it before and I have heard it. If it will expedite matters to have her tell it now, the defense is perfectly willing."

"Very well," Judge Elwell ruled; "there's a lot of hearsay here."

"It isn't hearsay at all," Maxine Edfield snapped. "I know what I know right from her own lips. She wanted to force Harmon Haslett into marriage, and she talked it over with me in advance."

"Talked what over with you?" Dillon asked.

"Talked over the fact that she was going to pretend to be pregnant, use the old racket to try and force Harmon to run away with her and get married."

"She told you this herself?"

"She told me that herself."

"But it didn't work, she didn't get married?" Dillon asked.

"It did not. Harmon Haslett might have fallen for it,

but the company had a troubleshooter, a man named Garland—who's sitting right there in the courtroom—and Mr. Garland put a thousand dollars in hundred-dollar bills in an envelope and sent it—"

"Now wait a minute," Dillon interrupted. "You don't know what Garland did of your own knowledge."

"Well, I know that she got the thousand dollars in hundred-dollar bills and right at that time young Harmon Haslett took a quick trip to Europe; and there Ellen Calvert was, left with a broken romance, a series of disappointments in her personal career, and a thousand dollars in cash. So she moved west and started over again."

"Did you hear from her after she left?" Dillon asked.

"I never heard a word from her."

"How did you happen to get in touch with her again?"

"Through Mr. Lovett, the lawyer."

"That is Mr. Lovett, sitting here in court?"

"Yes, sir."

"And what happened?"

"He started trying to trace Ellen Calvert and started looking back into her record to find the people she had known. He found that she had been very friendly with me at one time and came to me and asked me about her."

"And he told you where she was?"

"Yes; he had found her by using detectives, I believe."

"In any event, he brought you here to Los Angeles?"

"Yes."

"You may inquire," Dillon said.

"When did you first see the defendant after you arrived in Los Angeles?" Mason asked.

"Oh, all right," she said. "I know what you're trying to get at. I made a wrong identification. After all, I hadn't seen Ellen for twenty years and you had a ringer, a woman who was almost the spitting image of Ellen. You planted her on me so I made a wrong identification. But that was all that was wrong about my testimony. I just made a mistake about that woman. I *thought* she was Ellen Calvert, or Ellen Adair, as she calls herself now. But the minute I saw the real Ellen I was absolutely certain. I simply couldn't have been mistaken with *her*—but the way I was brainwashed on that identification, I *did* make a mistake with the first person I saw. But that was a deliberate plant and, anyway, all that was wrong was the identification. That didn't affect in any way the things that had happened twenty years ago or the things that Ellen had told me."

Judge Elwell said, "Even making allowances for the fact that this is a preliminary examination and that there is no objection on the part of counsel for either side, it seems to me that this witness is unduly garrulous and that it might be better to restrict the examination to question and answer."

"That's what I am doing. I'm answering questions," Maxine Edfield said. "But I know what he's going to try to do. He's going to try to discredit me because he ran this ringer in on me and I identified her. And then he trapped me into making the identification absolutely positive when, actually, I only *felt* the woman I had identified as Ellen was Ellen. I wasn't completely *sure* of it."

"But you said you were sure?" Mason asked.

"All right, I said I was sure, and I said I was just as certain of my identification as of any other part of my testimony. You trapped me. That's an old lawyer's trick. I know now because Mr. Lovett told me. But I didn't know it at the time. I hadn't had any experience with lawyers."

Judge Elwell said, "I'm going to ask the witness to just answer questions and stop—just answer what is required in order to give the information requested."

"Your expenses were paid by Mr. Lovett?" Mason asked.

"Yes, they were. Mr. Lovett came to me all open and aboveboard, and he wanted me to come out here with him, and I told him I was a working girl, and he said he would take care of my expenses."

"And he gave you money to cover expenses?"

"He gave me some money, yes."

"And you used that to pay expenses?"

"Well, some of them, and some of them he paid."

"You came with Mr. Lovett on the plane?"

"Yes."

"Who purchased the ticket for your transportation?"

"Mr. Lovett."

"When you came here you went to a hotel?"

"Yes."

"Mr. Lovett is staying at that same hotel?"

"Yes, he is."

"And who is paying the hotel bill at that hotel?"

"Why, Mr. Lovett, I suppose."

"And what about meals?"

"I either sign for meals in the hotel restaurant or I have my meals with Mr. Lovett or sometimes they are sent up to my room."

"Then how much actual expenses have you paid from the money Mr. Lovett gave you?"

"Well . . . just incidental expenses."

"How much?"

"I don't know."

"Have you kept an account?"

"Not a detailed account."

"And what are the incidental expenses?"

"Oh, little things that you can't charge—newspapers, beauty parlors, and little things like that."

"You haven't paid out fifty dollars in incidental expenses, have you?"

"Well, perhaps not."

"You haven't paid out twenty-five dollars."

"Perhaps not."

"You haven't paid out ten dollars."

"Well, perhaps not, but it probably is around that vicinity somewhere."

"And how much money did Mr. Lovett give you for expenses?"

"I don't think that has anything to do with it. That's a private matter between Mr. Lovett and me."

"How much money did Mr. Lovett give you for expenses?"

Maxine Edfield turned to Judge Elwell. "Do I have to answer that question?"

"I think it's a proper question. I have heard no objection to it. I think the prosecution considers it as proper cross-examination."

"All right," she blazed. "If you have to know, he gave me five hundred dollars."

"Five hundred dollars for incidental expenses," Mason said.

"Yes, that's right," she flared. "I had to leave my job and come out here."

"You got a leave of absence from your job, didn't you?"

"Well, I had a vacation coming."

"How much of a vacation?"

"Two weeks."

"And did Mr. Lovett arrange with your employer to extend your two-week vacation if necessary?"

"I don't know what he did. I know I'm out here on my own on a vacation."

"Then you are getting paid for your time out here?"

"All right, I'm entitled to it. If I want to spend my vacation out here, that's my business."

"Now, then," Mason said, "did Mr. Lovett offer you some sort of a bonus in case he was successful in his contention and in case your testimony was instrumental in winning his case?"

"He did not!"

"Didn't he tell you that if your evidence stood up in court his clients would be—"

"Well, that's different," she said. "That's something else again. You asked me about Mr. Lovett."

"But Mr. Lovett told you that his clients would be grateful?"

"Something like that."

"Very grateful?"

"Well, they certainly should be. There's a two-million-dollar estate involved, and they couldn't ever have found out the truth if it hadn't been for me and what Ellen told me."

Mason said, "You say there's a two-million-dollar estate involved?"

"That's right. Ezekiel Haslett, Harmon Haslett's father, died and left all of the stock in the Cloverville Spring and Suspension Company to Harmon. Then Harmon was on a yachting trip and the yacht was wrecked and there have been no survivors. There are two half brothers, Bruce and Norman Jasper, and I believe there's some funny sort of a will in which Harmon Haslett stated that he had reason to believe he might be the father of an illegitimate child and if that was the case he left all of his estate to the illegitimate child.

"Now, that's what you were going to try to drag out of me on cross-examination," the witness said defiantly. "Now I've told you all I know, and I've told you the truth."

The witness got up, preparing to leave the witness stand.

"Just a moment, just a moment," Mason said. "I haven't yet come to the point I wanted to bring out. Were you acquainted with Agnes Burlington in her lifetime?"

The witness dropped back into the witness stand, glared at Mason, averted her eyes, looked back at Mason, and said defiantly, "I had met her, yes."

"When did you meet her?"

"I met her on the evening of the third."

"Where?"

"At her duplex home."

"And how did you happen to go there?"

"Now, just a minute, just a minute," Dillon interrupted. "This is all news to the prosecution, and I object to it on the ground that it is not proper cross-examination. We did not bring out anything whatever about the relations of this witness with Agnes Burlington, and I think this part of the testimony is incompetent, irrelevant and immaterial."

"Well, I don't," Judge Elwell snapped. "If this witness, with her interest in the case, knew Agnes Burlington, I'd like to find out about it, and I'd like to find out what Agnes Burlington had to do with the case."

"Answer the question," Mason said.

"All right," Maxine Edfield said defiantly. "Mr. Lovett had detectives who had told him about Agnes Burlington, who had been a nurse in a hospital in San Francisco and had been in attendance at a time when a baby boy, who is now named Wight Baird, was born.

"Well, I heard that Ellen was going to rely on this Agnes Burlington to establish her fraudulent claim against the estate of Harmon Haslett.

"Well, I went to see her because I knew that anything she would testify to would be completely false. I wanted to tell her unmistakably and plainly right from the start that I knew Ellen Calvert had been just using the old razzle-dazzle on Harmon Haslett in order to make him think he was going to be a father."

"And you saw Agnes Burlington?"

"I saw her."

"Did you get anywhere with her?"

"I told her frankly that if she testified to the fact that

Ellen Calvert had had a child, I could prove she was a liar."

"What else?"

"That was all. She virtually threw me out, told me to mind my own business. The whole interview didn't take over ten minutes—but I warned her: I told her she could be convicted of perjury if she swore to those lies."

"What did she say to that?"

"Just told me to get out."

"I have no further question," Mason said.

"That's all," Dillon said, "and that concludes the testimony of the prosecution, except that I want to formally introduce in evidence the thirty-eight-caliber revolver which the police found in the glove compartment of the defendant's car."

Judge Elwell said, "I think there is no question that the circumstantial evidence here is sufficient to bind the defendant over. However, if Mr. Mason has any testimony . . ."

Mason arose deferentially. "If the Court pleases," he said, "I would like to call Mr. Paul Drake as my first witness."

"Very well. Mr. Drake, come forward and be sworn."

Mason examined Paul Drake. "Your name is Paul Drake. You are a duly licensed private detective and have, from time to time, been employed by me in connection with cases?"

"Yes, sir."

"Now I am going to ask you if, pursuant to my instructions, you found out where the decedent, Agnes Burlington, was accustomed to buying her groceries."

"I did; yes, sir."

"Directing your attention to the evening of the fourth of this month, do you know where Agnes Burlington purchased groceries?"

"On the late afternoon of the fourth," Paul Drake said, "Agnes Burlington purchased a frozen dinner at the Sunrise Special Supermarket, which is approximately two blocks from where she lived."

"Do you know what she purchased at that time?"

"I know only because of hearsay through talking with a Miss Donna Findley, who is one of the checkers at the market."

"Very well," Mason said; "I will ask you to step down and I will call Miss Donna Findley as my next witness."

Donna Findley, an attractive young woman in her early twenties, took the witness stand, was sworn, and gave her name and occupation.

"Were you acquainted with Agnes Burlington in her lifetime?" Mason asked.

"I was. I was quite friendly with her—that is, in a business way."

"What do you mean by in a business way?"

"I am a checker at the Sunrise Special Supermarket and Agnes Burlington bought groceries there quite frequently. She would usually check out at my counter, and we'd talk for a minute while I was adding up the total."

"Do you remember an occasion on the evening of the fourth?"

"Very well," she said.

"What happened?"

"Agnes bought a loaf of bread, a bar of butter, a carton of milk, and a frozen dinner, of the kind known as the TV Special."

"Do you know what was in the TV Special Dinner?"

"It was a scallop dinner, containing scallops, green peas, mashed potatoes, and a special sauce for the scallops."

"How do you happen to remember that?" Mason asked.

"We talked, and I asked her what she was eating that night, and she told me she was having one of the scallop dinners—that she had them from time to time and they were very nice."

"Thank you," Mason said. "You may inquire."

"Just this one particular evening," Dillon asked sarcastically, "you talked with Agnes Burlington about what she was going to eat?"

"No, I talked with her many times. Agnes lived by herself, and she used quite a bit of frozen food."

"You remember this was the fourth?"

"Very clearly, because I remember that I didn't see her on the fifth, and then on the sixth I heard about her death."

"What time was this on the fourth?"

"About five-thirty in the evening, perhaps a quarter to six."

"How do you fix the time?"

"I am off duty at eight o'clock and—well, I know generally what time it was."

"You can't fix the time accurately?"

"Not accurately. I know it was before eight o'clock on the evening of the fourth, and I would say it was about two hours or two hours and a half before I left work."

"No further question," Dillon said.

Mason said, "If the Court pleases, I would like to find out from Lieutenant Tragg if any search was made of the garbage or trash can of the Agnes Burlington duplex."

"For what purpose?" Judge Elwell asked.

"To show that the empty carton in which this dinner of scallops, green peas, and mashed potatoes had been contained was found in the garbage."

"That wouldn't prove anything," Dillon said. "Of course it was in the garbage. We now know that she bought a frozen dinner. We know the dinner was in her stomach. Therefore, the container must have been in the garbage. But we don't know *when* that dinner was consumed."

"The assumption would be that it was consumed that night. She told the witness, Donna Findley, that she was going to have it that night," Mason said.

"And she could have changed her mind," Dillon retorted. "But it doesn't make any real difference, anyway, because the mere fact that she was killed within a couple of hours after ingesting that dinner doesn't mean a thing."

"It does when one considers it in connection with the water which had been running," Mason said. "The water was left running all night."

"So what?" Dillon asked.

"So," Mason said, "when the defendant's car left tracks in the driveway it was at a time when the water had been running for many, many hours, indicating that Agnes Burlington was unable to turn off the water because she had been killed."

"It doesn't mean any such thing," Dillon said. "That's an elaborate, finespun theory. For all we know, that driveway could have been wet for several days or several nights. The autopsy surgeon says that death probably took place on the evening of the fourth, so all Mason is doing is dotting the i's and crossing the t's on the prosecution's testimony."

"The defense has an interesting theory here," Judge Elwell said, "but I don't think it can have any influence upon a committing magistrate. I can see where this theory could be worked into a very interesting interpretation of circumstantial evidence to be placed in front of a jury —and, of course, the rule of circumstantial evidence is that if there is any reasonable hypothesis other than that of guilt on which the circumstantial evidence can be logically explained, the jury is required to adopt that hypothesis and bring in a verdict of acquittal, if the case is founded entirely upon circumstantial evidence.

"However, that is neither here nor there as far as *this* Court is concerned. This Court is called upon only to determine whether a crime has been committed and whether there are reasonable grounds to connect the defendant with the crime."

Mason arose. "May I ask the indulgence of the Court?"

"Go ahead," Judge Elwell said, "but please don't argue the circumstantial evidence, because I don't think it has any place in this Court. It would seem that the evidence now before the Court is such that the defendant must be bound over."

Mason said, "I have not been given an opportunity to

make a detailed inspection of the premises. I would like to have the case continued until I can make such a detailed inspection."

"For what purpose?"

"The fact that the fatal bullet was never found is indicative of the fact that something may have been overlooked."

Dillon said sarcastically, "Do you expect you can find something which was overlooked by the police?"

"I can try," Mason said. "At least I should have the right."

Judge Elwell hesitated for a few moments, then said, "It would seem to me that the request is reasonable. The defense cannot uncover any evidence which would be persuasive as far as this Court is concerned; but, on the other hand, it is quite possible that there is evidence which might be of tremendous importance in connection with a jury trial."

Dillon said, "We object to it, Your Honor. The defendant, accompanied by the defendant's attorney and his secretary, saw the premises when they discovered the body of the decedent."

"And were careful not to touch anything but notified the police right away," Judge Elwell said. "Now the body has been removed and supposedly all of the evidence has been uncovered, and it would certainly seem that the defendant's attorney is entitled to make a detailed inspection of the premises."

"We object to it," Dillon said.

"Why do you object to it, Mr. Prosecutor?"

"Because Counsel is well known for being ingenious and his methods are unconventional."

"What could he possibly do at this late date?" Judge Elwell asked.

"Suppose he took a revolver with him and found some obscure corner of the room, or perhaps a louver in a ventilator, and fired a bullet and then claimed that this was evidence which had been overlooked by the police?"

"That is tantamount to an accusation of unprofessional conduct," Judge Elwell said.

"I am making no accusations, but I may say that the police are not finished with the premises as yet."

"Why not?" Mason asked. "Do you think there is further evidence which hasn't been uncovered?"

"I don't know," Dillon said, "but, as you yourself have remarked, the fact that there is no evidence of the fatal bullet might be significant. Therefore, the police have sealed up the premises just as they found things. We would like to keep them intact, at least until after this hearing."

Judge Elwell said, "I'm going to make this suggestion. The Court wants to look at the premises to see if there is any possibility that a hole made by the fatal bullet could have been overlooked. From the angle of the shot, it is possible to find that bullet almost anywhere—even in the ceiling."

"The police have looked in the ceiling. They have looked everywhere," Dillon said.

"Then there is no reason why the premises should be kept sealed up," Judge Elwell remarked.

"This Court is going to take a two-hour recess. During that time we will go to the premises and inspect them. The defendant's attorney will be given every opportunity to inspect the premises, and I would like to have the prosecutor and Lieutenant Tragg present during the inspection so that the Court can question them.

"The Court will also ask the Court reporter to be in attendance and take down anything that is said."

"Such an inspection can't do any good," Dillon protested.

"Well, can it do any harm?" Judge Elwell asked.

Dillon started to say something, then changed his mind.

"It is so ordered," Judge Elwell said. "Court will take a recess and reconvene at the scene of the murder. We will ask the sheriff's office to furnish transportation."

Chapter Seventeen

Lieutenant Tragg stood in the middle of the room, acting somewhat as master of ceremonies.

"Your Honor will notice that the place where the body was found has been outlined in chalk," he said. "There is also an outline in red chalk of the pool of blood.

"I may state that the strong probabilities are that the fatal bullet was carried out in this pool of blood, which unfortunately happens altogether too frequently.

"The bullet has just enough force to leave the body and fall to the floor, the blood flows over the bullet and, in the course of a few hours, coagulates into a gelatinous mass.

"The police outline the position of the body. They outline the pool of blood. They take photographs, and then the body is removed and the blood is removed in the form of one large clot. It sometimes happens that the fatal bullet is imbedded somewhere in this blood clot.

"At other times, the fatal bullet is in the clothing of the decedent and falls out when the body is moved and either is lost or is found in the ambulance. But when a bullet is found in an ambulance there is not very much that can be done with it since it can't be identified as having come from any particular body.

"I can assure Your Honor that these things happen. They only happen at intervals, and they shouldn't happen at all, but they do happen."

Judge Elwell looked around the room. "Everything here has been left just as it was found?"

"Everything."

"You have examined the ceiling and . . ."

"We have examined every nook and corner of this room with a powerful spotlight," Lieutenant Tragg said. "Believe me, we would like very much to recover that fatal bullet. We think it would clinch the case."

Judge Elwell pursed his lips thoughtfully.

"What about the windows?" Mason asked.

"The windows were found just as you see them. They were locked from the inside and the drapes were tightly drawn. The evidence in the bathroom indicates the decedent was preparing to take a bath and had taken off her dress, thus accounting for the closed drapes. The windows were probably kept locked. We sealed everything in the room so there could be no mistake and no misunderstanding."

"But suppose a window had been up *at the time of the murder?*" Mason said. "The bullet could have gone out the open window."

"Yes, I suppose so," Tragg said, "and then the murderer would very obligingly have closed and locked the window."

"The weather records," Mason said, "show that there was a sudden thunderstorm sweeping this section of the city from eight twenty-five to eight fifty-five on the evening of the fourth. I don't know that it is particularly pertinent, but I have had my detective agency search for any event out of the ordinary which took place on that evening.

"These sudden severe thunderstorms are very infrequent in this locality."

"Well, what does a thunderstorm have to do with it?" Lieutenant Tragg asked.

"It might have to do with the closed windows," Mason said. "The weather reports show that the night was very humid, hot and oppressive. I note that there is no air conditioning in this house. Therefore, one would expect to have found the windows open, unless they were closed because of the thunderstorm."

"Not when a woman is taking or about to take a bath," Lieutenant Tragg said. "She would pull the drapes."

"A bullet could not have gone through the drapes without leaving a hole. There is no hole."

"All of this doesn't mean anything," Dillon interposed. "The decedent could well have been alive at the time the thunderstorm occurred and could have put down the windows, which had been open prior to that time. She could have been killed several hours later, at two or three o'clock in the morning, as far as that's concerned."

"Judging from the manner in which the decedent was dressed," Mason pointed out, "it is hardly possible that death would have occurred in the small hours of the morning. I suggest that we pull back the drapes, raise these windows, and take a look at the lower part of the window sash."

"What good is that going to do?" Dillon asked.

Judge Elwell was frowning thoughtfully.

"It might do a lot of good," Mason said. "It would fix the time of death. There is a very good chance that Agnes Burlington was engaged in the act of closing a window when she was shot."

"About one chance in ten million," Dillon said.

"No," Mason said, "the chances are very good. Let us assume that Agnes Burlington had some visitor who was threatening her. She was holding a gun in her hand. A thunderstorm sent great gusts of wind and rain coming in the window on the west, billowing the drapes into the room. She went over to close the window, and the moment she turned her back on her visitor, the visitor whipped out a gun and shot her.

"That would account for the so-called upward course of the bullet in the body. It would mean that the decedent, while closing the window, was actually bent over with her back partially turned to the murderer and that the drapes, blown by the sudden violent gust of wind, were billowing inward so they weren't in the path of the bullet."

"Here we go," Dillon said; "one of these fantastic, far-fetched theories for which Counsel is noted, twisting the circumstantial evidence into a bizarre pattern of events, confusing the issues, and, in general, distorting everything in the case. All right, Ellen Adair could have killed Agnes Burlington at the moment the first gust of wind from the thunderstorm hit the open window and billowed the drapes, and that could have been thirty minutes after the decedent ate her scallops and peas—and we still haven't proven anything."

"Just the same," Judge Elwell said, "that theory interests me. When we have a case where the police can't find the fatal bullet which undoubtedly emerged from the body of the decedent, Counsel is certainly entitled to explore all the possibilities. Lieutenant Tragg, I'd like to have the drapes pulled back and that window raised, please."

Lieutenant Tragg pulled the drapes, raised the window.

Judge Elwell leaned forward to examine the lower part of the sash and the screen.

"What's this, Lieutenant?" Judge Elwell asked.

Lieutenant Tragg examined the lower screen where a small hole had been concealed by the lower part of the window sash.

"There seems to be a small hole in the screen. There's nothing to show the cause."

"That could have been made by a bullet?" Judge Elwell asked.

Lieutenant Tragg hesitated.

"And it could have been made by an astute individual who wanted to confuse the issue," Dillon exploded. "This whole thing is too coincidental, altogether too pat to suit me."

Judge Elwell regarded him thoughtfully. "It never occurred to you to raise the window and look at the lower part of the screen that was concealed by the bottom of the window?"

"Certainly not. The body was discovered in this room with all the windows closed and locked and the drapes drawn."

"Under the circumstances," Judge Elwell said, "and in view of the peculiar course of the wound in the body, indicating that the shot had been fired from a low angle or, more logically, that it had been fired while the decedent was bending over, as would have been the case in closing a window of this sort, I think it was incumbent upon the police department to have investigated this phase of the case.

"The fact that it was suggested by Mr. Mason doesn't make it any the less logical and, in view of this evidence which we have now discovered, I think the police should carry on a further investigation for the purpose of trying to locate that fatal bullet.

"If Mr. Mason is correct in his theory, the fatal shot was fired while the decedent was half turning, trying to keep someone covered with the gun she was holding and, at the same time, to lower the window. The murderer, whoever he or she was, took advantage of that moment to whip out a gun and fire the fatal shot.

"Agnes Burlington, in all probability, had no idea that the person she was holding at the point of her revolver was armed.

"After Agnes Burlington fell to the floor, her murderer stepped over the body, finished closing the window and locked it."

"There is no evidence that this little hole in the screen was caused by a bullet," Dillon objected.

"Then what *did* cause it?" Judge Elwell asked.

"It could have been caused by anything. It could have been caused by *someone*"—and here Dillon looked accusingly at Perry Mason—"taking a small piece of pipe, holding it against the screen, and hitting the end of the pipe a sharp blow with a hammer."

"Possibly," Judge Elwell said, "but in view of the fact that the police have had this place sealed and the seals have not been tampered with, it would seem that the prosecution is now the side that is indulging in fanciful theories.

"I suggest to the police that a search be made of the ground outside of this window, and for a distance of some feet, to see if this bullet can be recovered.

"I am going to continue the case until tomorrow morning at ten o'clock to give the police an opportunity to make this search. I may say that if a fatal bullet is recovered, it should be determinative. If it came from the gun found in the glove compartment of the defendant's car, it will be a most significant piece of evidence. If, on the other hand, it did *not* come from that weapon, this Court is going to take another good long look at the evidence.

"I think that's all we need to do here. The police have searched every nook and cranny. There was only the one place that wasn't searched, and that place seems to have been the one which held the significant clue.

"Court will stand adjourned until tomorrow morning at ten o'clock."

Chapter Eighteen

PERRY MASON moved over to Lieutenant Tragg's side as they filed from the duplex house.

"Want to listen?" he asked.

"I'm a listener," Tragg said.

Mason said, "When I am taken back to my office, why not come up with me?"

"It's a deal," Tragg told him.

"And," Mason said, "I would suggest you say nothing to Dillon."

Tragg said, "I would just as soon avoid Mr. Dillon for a while. As a matter of fact, Perry, my face is red. I overlooked a bet.

"We wanted to leave that murder room just exactly the way it was. We found the windows closed, and that window on the west was locked. Therefore, I made a note that it was a locked window and we sealed the place with strips of paper so the evidence couldn't be disturbed without breaking the seal. That probably was good practice, but when I couldn't find the fatal bullet I should have done a little more thinking, I guess."

The little group of lawyers, courtroom attachés and police officers entered the transportation furnished by the sheriff's office, to be delivered to their respective destinations. Lieutenant Tragg left to join Perry Mason in the lawyer's office.

"All right, Mason," Tragg said, "go ahead and shoot."

"There are entries in Agnes Burlington's diary that are rather cryptic but furnish corroborating evidence that she was blackmailing the defendant."

"Go ahead," Tragg said.

"We've gone at this case backwards," Mason said. "We've been looking at it from the standpoint of the defendant."

"How should we have looked at it?"

"From the standpoint of the decedent."

"And what would that give us?"

"Suppose," Mason said, "you were a blackmailer. You've been blackmailing a woman over the birth of an illegitimate child. You've been getting chicken feed. All of a sudden you find yourself in a position where your testimony is the key testimony in an estate involving two million dollars. What are you going to do? Are you going to sit idle?"

Lieutenant Tragg looked at Mason thoughtfully, blinking his eyes as he digested Mason's remarks. Suddenly he said, "Hell, no! If I'm a blackmailer, I'm going to try to cash in."

"Exactly," Mason said. "Agnes Burlington was a blackmailer. She decided to cash in.

"Now let's suppose she had some bits of documentary evidence that she had been holding in reserve, also some old .35 mm shots. Let us suppose she tried to cash in with someone who was as hard-boiled as she was. They came to a showdown. The price Agnes wanted was too much for this individual to pay. But, in trying to get her price, Agnes had disclosed the devastating nature of the evidence she held.

"Now you know and I know that a really good 'cat' burglar tries to do his stuff when his victim is in the bathtub or in the bathroom getting ready for a bath. The sound of running water while the tub is being filled, the splashing after a person gets in the tub, and the fact that a person bathes in the nude are determining factors.

"The big hotels are troubled with 'cat' burglars who put through an early-morning call to some person and then say it's a mistake. The roomer is wide awake and a little angry—too angry to go back to sleep. He gets up, goes to the bathroom, and starts the water running.

"The 'cat' burglar, who has been waiting outside the room, sneaks in, helps himself quickly to what he wants, and gets out. The roomer doesn't have any idea anything is wrong until he has occasion to pay for something. Then he opens his wallet and finds the money is all gone. It's a problem the big hotels have to wrestle with.

"That's what happened in this case. Agnes was ready to take a bath. She had turned the water on in the bathroom. This person who had been carefully planning the burglary was probably waiting behind the back door, which he had opened with a skeleton key.

"But Agnes heard a noise and wasn't too modest, so she threw the door open and caught the intruder right in the act. Agnes had a gun. She didn't think she was going to have to use it, but she had it and was holding her visitor at arm's length with that gun.

"A thunderstorm came up. A sudden gust of wind blew the drapes into the room so that Agnes in her near nudity was exposed to view from the street. Feminine-like, and almost instinctively, she reached for the window to slam it shut. Her visitor saw an opportunity and fired, then took possession of the evidence which could have cost one side of the case a couple of million dollars."

"You got any ideas about that visitor?" Tragg said.

"Let's use a little logic there," Mason said. "The visitor was someone who carried a gun. That visitor went to the interview not intending to shoot, not anticipating that Agnes Burlington would pull a thirty-two-caliber revolver —perhaps not anticipating that the evidence that Agnes Burlington had was quite as devastating as turned out to be the case.

"The visitor was someone who would normally have carried a gun, who was vitally interested in the two million dollars, probably working on a contingency basis with the half brothers."

"You mean the attorney representing them?" Tragg asked skeptically.

"Attorneys don't carry guns," Mason said. "Who carries guns?"

"Police officers," Tragg said, "but that doesn't mean anything."

"And private detectives," Mason said. "We have a Jarmen Dayton in the case who is a private detective, who is—"

Tragg snapped his fingers.

"An ordinary murderer," Mason went on, "could get rid of the murder weapon, but a private detective who is licensed to carry a gun might have a little more difficulty disposing of a gun. He couldn't explain not having his gun.

"While your men are searching for that fatal bullet, Tragg, why don't you pay an official call on Jarmen Dayton, ask to see the gun he is carrying, check his credentials, fire a couple of test bullets from that gun, and then, in case you do uncover a fatal bullet, see if they match?"

Lieutenant Tragg thought the matter over. "I'm sticking my neck way, way, way out," he said.

"What do you have to lose?" Mason asked.

"Well, Dayton could make a complaint that I'd been unduly suspicious."

"And what do you have to win if you're right?" Mason asked.

Tragg thought that over.

"A spectacular solution of a murder case which has attracted a lot of attention," Mason pointed out; "a two-million-dollar estate . . ."

Tragg held up his hand. "Forget it," he said; "you win."

The telephone jangled sharply.

Della Street picked up the instrument, said, "Just a minute." Then she said to Mason, "The operator says she has an important message sent at double urgent rates."

"Who's it from?" Mason asked.

"Just a minute," Della Street said, her pencil flying over her notebook as the message was read over the telephone.

"Yes, I have it," Della Street said.

Della Street looked up at Mason and said, "Answering your question as to whom the message is from, it seems to be from Harmon Haslett. The message is from the Azores. It states that he was shipwrecked; that after swimming for hours in a life jacket he was picked up by the crew of a small fishing boat which had no wireless; that he has just been landed at the Azores; that he has heard news that you are involved in a suit concerning the contents of his will; that he is taking the first jet available and will be here sometime tomorrow."

Lieutenant Tragg said, "Well, I'll . . . be . . . damned!"

Mason said to Della Street, "Don't tell Gertie anything about this."

"Why?"

"You know how romantic Gertie is. Fancy how she will start anticipating what's going to happen when Harmon Haslett meets his sweetheart of twenty years ago, the mother of his illegitimate child—a woman, incidentally, whom he had never forgotten—a son that he didn't know he had, whose existence he only suspected."

"And the queenly Ellen Adair," Della Street said. "What will happen to *her* composure?"

Mason turned to Lieutenant Tragg. "If you'll get busy on that fatal bullet and rounding up Jarmen Dayton's gun, Lieutenant, there's just a possibility that Ellen Adair will be released from custody by the time Harmon Haslett gets here."

"You do put me in the damnedest situations." Tragg grinned and then, after a moment, asked, "Are you going to give out the terms of this message to the press?"

"No," Mason said, "you are. This is part of the credit you get in return for your cooperation."

Tragg hesitated a moment, then extended his right hand. "Sometimes you make me mad, Perry," he said, "but right now I'm moving you to the head of the table."

Chapter Nineteen

PROMPTLY at ten o'clock Judge Elwell opened the door from his chambers and ascended the bench.

"Everyone stand," the bailiff said.

The packed courtroom stood at breathless attention.

Judge Elwell seated himself. The bailiff rapped with his gavel. "Be seated. Court is now in session."

Judge Elwell said, "The People versus Ellen Calvert, alias Ellen Adair.

"The Court feels that, in view of the action which the Court is about to take, there should be a statement of facts so that there will be no misunderstanding as to the reason for the Court's action or what is being done.

"When the police entered the room in which the murder had been committed, they were confronted with windows which were closed and locked, drapes which were fully drawn. In order to preserve the evidence as they found it, the police sealed these windows, and it appeared that the windows were never raised until yesterday when, at the suggestion of counsel for the defense, the window on the west was raised and it immediately became apparent that some object, presumably a bullet, had left a hole in the lower part of the screen, a part concealed by the lower sash of the closed window.

"A search of the premises outside the window—a search facilitated by digging up the surface of the soil in a long strip, then subjecting that soil to a gold-mining process—disclosed what police now feel certain is the fatal bullet.

"A new suspect has entered the case—the private detective from Cloverville named Jarmen Dayton. The fatal bullet found by police apparently came from his gun.

"A search warrant issued out of this Court, and under which the baggage of Jarmen Dayton was searched, brought about the disclosure of documents in the handwriting of the decedent, Agnes Burlington, and .35 mm shots which apparently were taken from the possession of the decedent at the time of the murder.

"Under the circumstances, this Court feels that it has no alternative except to dismiss the case against Ellen Adair.

"While in a preliminary examination of this sort the Court usually confines itself to reviewing the evidence to see if there is sufficient evidence to justify binding the defendant over for trial and does not concern itself with the question of guilt or innocence of the defendant, the Court, in this case, is so convinced that the murder of Agnes Burlington was the result of the criminal activities of persons other than the defendant that there is no alternative except to dismiss the case. The Court, therefore, dismisses the case against Ellen Calvert, alias Ellen Adair, and she is released from custody."

A wild tumult of applause broke out in the courtroom. In vain, Judge Elwell tried to control the audience; then, with a faint smile, he arose from the bench.

It was at that time that the door from the corridor burst open and a tall man came racing down the aisle.

Ellen Adair, standing in queenly dignity, smiling faintly at the enthusiastic audience, suddenly stiffened to attention; her eyes widened as the man pushed his way through the crowd down the aisle and reached her side.

"Ellen!" he exclaimed.

Ellen tried to keep her voice calm, but there was a faint tremor. "Hello, Harmon," she said.

Harmon hesitated for a moment, then suddenly, as his eyes fastened on Wight Baird, who had come to stand by his mother's side, said, "You don't need to tell me, Ellen. He's the spitting image of his grandfather, Ezekiel Haslett."

Ellen let out a long breath. "I think," she said, "he needs a father's discipline."

It was at that point that Harmon Haslett reached out, took Ellen Adair in his arms, and held her close while the flashlights of newspaper photographers flooded the courtroom with brilliance.

Mason grinned at Della Street.

"I think," the lawyer said, "this is where we came in."